David scowled, an unusual expression for him. "Who touched the door?"

"I did."

"Advice for the future: Don't touch doors in the demon realm unless you want them to know you're here."

Dane ducked his head, his ears reddening. "It's warded?"

"Yes. How can you assume the mirror's warded, but not think the door it's behind is?"

I0538070

Discord Jones

Black Magic Shadows

Gayla Drummond

Katarr Kanticles Press

This is a work of fiction. Names, characters, places and incidents either are the products of the author's imagination or used fictitiously, and any resemblance to actual persons, living or dead, business establishments, events, or locales is entirely coincidental.

Katarr Kanticles Press
Texas, USA
Edited by Tonya Cannariato
Copyright © 2014 Gayla Drummond
Cover by Gayla Drummond

ISBN-13: 978-0692461297 (Katarr Kanticles Press)
ISBN-10: 0692461299

Acknowledgments

Super big thanks to you, the reader!
Without you, this series wouldn't have happened.

ONE

The day after Christmas, and no rest for the vampire-haunted. I resisted the urge to check my hair, uncomfortable with the scrutiny of our new client. Lady Celadine was an elf, a willowy blonde with piercing, grass-green eyes. Beautiful, check. Snooty? I was waiting for evidence. She had yet to respond to my "How may we help you?"

Mr. Whitehaven hadn't sent any information prior to the meeting, which was unusual. Dane had pulled a chair to the left end of my desk. My partner hadn't made his usual offer of coffee or another drink, either.

Finally Lady Celadine sniffed.

"Is there a problem?"

"I thought you'd be more attractive."

Boy, this was going to be fun.

"After all, the Prince seems quite taken with you," she said. "I can't think why."

My new delusion, lounging against the closed door, laughed. Snooty, check. "That makes two of us. Now, how can we help you?"

She frowned. "One of my belongings has been stolen. A mirror."

Okay. I could see the loss of a mirror being a huge issue for her. "Was it stolen from your sidhe?"

"Of course not."

"Arrogant bitch," Merriven murmured, and I had to stop myself from agreeing with him. Agreeing with a delusion had to be one of the steps to complete insanity. I was trying not to go there, since I preferred jackets with normal-length sleeves.

"Where was this mirror stolen from?"

"The museum."

Gah, trying to get information from her was like trying to get blood from a turnip. "Why was your mirror at the museum?"

Lady Celadine lifted her chin and arched her perfect eyebrows. "Why are items typically in museums?"

Guess I'd walked into that one. "To be displayed for public viewing. That doesn't completely answer my question, though. Why was your particular mirror being displayed?"

"It wasn't yet on display."

Oh, good night. "We need information if we're going to find your mirror. What's special about it, that someone would steal it?"

"The museum was planning to display it as part of the Fairy Tales Come to Life collection. The mirror houses a spirit."

"Wait, I know this one: Snow White. Her evil queen stepmother had a magic mirror. Right?"

A faint sneer appeared on her face. "Human fairy tales."

I'd had just about enough of her. "Okay, we'll start working on it, and let you know when we have any progress to report."

Up went her chin again. If someone ever shared the truth with the elves that their noble features deteriorated to ridiculous when they looked down their noses, they'd probably quit doing it. I wasn't about to inform her.

"You're not at all the type of human woman I'd expect Thorandryll to find attractive."

As insults went, that was one I could shrug off. "I've thought the exact same thing." Rising from my chair, I smiled. "Dane will see you out."

Lady Celadine cast a disdainful glance at my partner. "I don't require the assistance of an animal."

Grr. "Bully for you. Bye."

With a series of sniffs, she stood and left, leaving my office door open. Merriven had disappeared before she'd reached it.

"Not liking the new client," I said once she'd left the building.

"That makes two of us." Dane rolled his eyes. "Elves."

"Yeah." I checked the time on my desktop monitor. Nearly noon. "I'm meeting Mom for lunch. What are we doing after?"

"Why are you asking me?"

"Because you're lead on this case."

Dane grinned. "Really?" When I nodded, he said, "Cool. Let's meet at the museum, check things out there. They probably have photos of the mirror, and maybe there's security footage."

"Sounds like a plan. I'll meet you there."

He stood and moved the chair he'd been sitting on back into its usual spot in front of my desk, before saying, "Hey."

"Yeah?" I grabbed my purse and coat. All the snow had melted away, but it was still cold.

"Is everything okay?"

"Hunky dory." I was such a liar, but I didn't want to tell my friends I was worried I was going crazy. Instead, I planned to tell my mom, and see what she thought I should do to find out if I really was.

"Okay. Just wondering. You and Logan were getting cozy, then nothing since Solstice. You haven't even visited us, and we're like, right there. Neighbors."

Guilt sucked. "I know. I've got something I have to take care of. Nothing major." Just possibly losing my mind.

Dane nodded. "You know we'll help, if we can."

How had I gotten so damn lucky in the friends category? "I know. But I have to do this myself."

"Okay. I guess I'll see you at the museum."

"Yep." I left my office ahead of him, nodding to Tabitha on my way out. I was liking our receptionist, who had a penchant for wearing faux, fuzzy animal ears via headbands. Once seated behind the wheel of my 280 ZX, I sighed. Being a psychic kind of sucked a lot at the moment.

"Oh, come now," Merriven said from the passenger seat. "You're young and powerful. The world is yours for the taking, lovely child."

"If I take over the world, will you go the hell away?"

The vampire smiled. "No. I have no plans to ever leave you for long."

Great. I buckled my seatbelt and started my car. Lana Del Ray's "Dark Paradise" softly moaned out of the speakers. I glared at the stereo. "I did not buy that song."

"You did, at my suggestion. It's glorious, and oh so appropriate for us, don't you think?"

"That's it. I'm not speaking to you anymore." My finger trembled as I punched stereo buttons to select a different song. Dad and Betty had given me a computer for Christmas, with a year's worth of Internet service. I'd spent the evening before buying MP3s for the memory stick currently plugged into the stereo's USB port. And I did not remember picking that song. Didn't even remember Merriven appearing in my home office while I was music shopping.

TWO

My mom was just leaving her car when I pulled into the parking lot of the café we'd agreed on. She waved and pointed to the front door, to let me know she'd wait inside.

I waved back and nodded, before finding a parking space.

"Dear, delicious Sunny."

"Shut up, fang face." He hadn't bitten Mom while holding her hostage. Crap, I'd talked to him again. "Go away."

I left my car, shivering at a blast of cold wind that sent dust swirling across the parking lot, and went inside. Mom greeted me with a smile and a hug.

"Hi, Mom." My courage failed. I knew I needed to talk to someone, but maybe she wasn't the best choice after all. Merriven had terrorized her.

"Hello. It feels like a soup day, doesn't it?"

"It does." The gray clouds hiding the sun weren't helping anything, especially my mood. At least the café was brightly lit, and had an abundance of plants for decoration. We picked a table in a corner, where a couple of potted palm trees offered some privacy.

Once seated, she gave me an expectant look. "Out with it, young lady."

"What?"

"You want advice. Right? About what? Maybe Logan? I like him. He's a nice man. A little older, but maybe that's what you ne..."

"I think I'm going crazy," I blurted, and her eyes widened as she slowly closed her mouth.

"Let's order, and then you can tell me why you think that."

Melting into my seat, I nodded. "Okay."

After we'd ordered—Mom went with pho, while I picked that and a small order of veggie sushi—she scooted closer to the table and rested her arm on it, offering her hand. I took hold, careful not to squeeze too hard. Quietly, she said, "Tell me."

"I started seeing Ginger about a month ago. Not just in nightmares, but while I was awake."

"Her spirit?"

"I don't know. Don't think so. I mean, no one else noticed her, and if it was her ghost, surely someone would have mentioned something." After all, my friends were mostly witches and supes.

Mom pursed her lips. "Is she here now?"

I shook my head. "I don't see her anymore. The last time I saw her while I was awake, she helped me. She looked normal then, wasn't a vampire. But I saw her in a dream after that, and not since then."

Her eyebrows drew together. "If you haven't seen her again, I don't understand why..."

"Someone else has taken her place." I took a breath. "Merriven."

Mom's fingers tightened around mine. "He's dead."

"So is Ginger," I pointed out.

"Right, but," Mom sighed. "When did you begin seeing him?"

I waited to answer because our food was ready. After we had everything, I answered her question. "Solstice night. He walked out of the bonfire, after I tossed my wishes in." I scowled. "And he talks. Ginger didn't talk except in my dreams."

Mom pointed at my bowl of pho. "Eat before it gets cold."

Realizing she wanted time to think, I began collecting veggies and broth, and blew on the spoonful before tasting it.

"It was traumatic, what happened because of him," Mom eventually said. "It's not surprising you'd have nightmares about him."

"Not just nightmares."

"Seeing him when you're awake doesn't mean you're crazy, Cordi. There's a saying that crazy people don't know they're crazy."

My head tilted as I looked at her. "Are you seriously handing out clichés right now?"

She smiled. "People who see or hear things others don't..."

"Remember that thing? What was it?" I snapped my fingers. "Oh, yeah, the Melding. There are loads of people who do things others can't, Mom, including seeing and hearing things. Me, for example."

"I am really losing my touch with analogies."

"Yeah, kind of."

She chuckled, but quickly sobered. "There has to be a reason you're seeing him, and it doesn't have to be related to your sanity. You've always felt guilty about Ginger. Having to face Merriven must've pushed it to the surface."

My mother could hit an emotional bull's eye without trying. I nodded. "He told me something."

"What?"

"He said he made her tell me those things."

Instant understanding dampened her eyes. "Oh, Cordi. But you didn't know that. It's not your fault."

"Doesn't make anything better."

Mom blinked. "He may have lied. You did say he managed to break into your mind."

"Yeah, he could've lied, but I won't ever know."

"Of course you will. You're having a problem with a vampire, so ask another one for help." Mom's smile was bright. "Derrick's nice. After all, how many vampires would think to bring someone flowers to wish them well? I'm sure he'd be willing to help."

Crap. I'd thought the same thing, but had hoped to avoid taking that route. No clue what it might involve. Derrick dipping into my mind seemed likely, and I wasn't ready to go that far with our relatively new friendship. Wow, I had a vampire friend. Two, even. "You really think that's what I should do?"

"It makes sense. He's an expert on vampires." She reached across the table to pat my hand. "Call him. It won't hurt to ask. At the least, he may be able to suggest something else."

"Okay. I will." My reluctance was apparent, because Mom raised her eyebrow. "I promise."

She leveled her patented Mom stare at me before saying, "Today."

Ugh. "Yes, today."

"Good."

It wasn't until I watched her leaving the parking lot that I realized she hadn't asked if I were seeing Merriven while we had lunch. Damn it, I'd probably dredged up things she hadn't wanted to think about. All of the relief I felt over finally talking to someone drained away. "I'm the worst daughter in the history of bad daughters."

"She'll dream of me tonight," Merriven said. "You're both wrong. That sniveling boy can't help you. No one can."

I ignored him, and left to meet Dane at the museum.

Santo Trueno only had one acknowledged museum, and I'd gone there a few times as a child, on school field trips. The building wasn't much to look at, a two-story slab of taupe in a T-shape, the long part hidden by the bar, which faced the parking lot. A couple of school buses waited, and there were a few other vehicles. I parked next to Dane's blue truck. My partner was waiting inside, checking out the gift shop offerings.

I was fifteen minutes late. "Sorry."

"No problem. How was lunch?"

"Healthy. You wouldn't have liked it, Lord of Pizza."

His grin surfaced. "Wheat germ and tofu?"

"I have an abiding dislike of tofu."

Dane put his hand on his chest and widened his eyes. "A food exists that you don't like? Call the media."

"Shut up. You're going to give me a complex." I'd been eating way too much comfort food lately.

"A complex about what? Tofu?"

"Eating."

He dropped his hand, wrinkling his nose. "Humans are so weird about food. Always worried about getting fat."

His comment struck a nerve. It wasn't as though I'd have my youthful metabolism forever. I'd also been given a hard time back in my younger school days, because I liked to eat. "Dude, quit."

"It's weird. Do you know we used to envy fat people, before the Melding? Even shifters can starve to death. Fat meant prosperous, and prosperous people lived through winters." Watching my face, Dane quickly added, "Not that I think you're fat. I didn't say I think you're fat. Just saying it's not a big deal to us."

"Yeah, okay, time to change the topic." And get serious about a workout routine. I didn't need extra weight slowing me down. Not in my line of work. I should start jogging. The dogs would like that. I wouldn't, but oh well.

"Sorry."

"New topic. What's our first step here?"

"Find out who's in charge." Which is exactly what we did, by asking the elderly lady behind the gift shop's register.

"This is where the mirror was." Tanisha Wills, the museum employee we'd been handed off to, after verifying who we were to the museum director, pointed to the corner of the room.

"Just propped there, or what?"

She shook her head. "No, it's a full-length mirror, with a carved frame and stand. No wheels, and let me tell you, it's a heavy sucker."

"So more than one person needed," I said.

Tanisha smiled, her teeth movie-star white. She was a striking, dark-skinned woman with close-cropped, natural hair. Amazing bone structure, and she was taller than me, too. "It took two elves to carry it in. Humans? Four of us to move it to the corner, and believe you me, we struggled doing it."

"Why the corner?" Dane looked up from the table he was perusing.

"The mirror is a perverted son of a bitch. He kept making sexual remarks. We moved him to the corner, and I threw a dust cloth over him."

"Did that work?"

"Well enough," she replied. "His owner needs to rethink letting him watch premium channels."

I looked around. "Nothing else was taken?"

"Just the mirror."

Huh. There were several more portable items lying on the three tables, as well as on the built-in shelving on each wall. Plenty of pretty, shiny stuff that looked more interesting than an old mirror housing a social miscreant. In fact... "Are those Cinderella's glass slippers?"

"Not glass. Crystal, and yes. Well, not exactly hers, but some elf lady's." Tanisha drew up her top lip a bit. "Trust me, even the Grimm versions were nicer than the true stories."

"I believe you. Who discovered the mirror was missing?"

"I did. I'm heading the team preparing the exhibit. It was there the afternoon of Christmas Eve, and gone when I unlocked the doors this morning."

Which meant Lady Celadine hadn't wasted any time hiring us. Interesting.

"Ooh, a locked door mystery." Dane left the table that had held his attention. "Be more interesting to solve if it weren't for magic."

"Yeah. Where's the dust cloth?" There wasn't anything in the room for me to try psychometry on. I checked the ceiling. "And is there a security camera in here?"

Tanisha chuckled. "There is, and guess what?"

"It went on the fritz."

"That's what they said, when I had the guys check. I can show you to the security room, if you want to see the video?"

"Yes, please." Maybe we'd notice something useful. "And if you have photos of the mirror, those would be really useful."

"Sure, I'll get you copies, and find the dust cloth for you."

The two daytime security guards on duty watching the cameras were in their sixties. I wondered if they ever had to run after art thieves or vandals as one offered me his chair. "Have a seat, miss."

"Thank you." I sat while the other guard clicked around on a monitor to pull up the video we wanted to see. My cell phone rang, playing the first notes of "Hotel California", and I popped out of my chair. "Have to take this call. I'll be right back."

I answered while hurrying out of the room, and walked down the hallway to make sure I would have some privacy. "Hi, sorry to have bothered you."

"You haven't," Derrick replied. "I have an obligation this evening. Would seven tomorrow evening be convenient for you?"

"That would be great." I'd called from my car earlier, and hadn't expected such a quick meeting. "I mean, if you're sure it's not..."

"It's no trouble, and if you like, you're welcome to join us for dinner." He paused. "Stone, that is."

"Ah, sure. Thank you."

"We'll see you at seven then."

"Thanks, bye." I ended the call and hoped I wasn't making a big mistake. Trusting a vampire had never been on any of my To Do lists. Of course, Lord Derrick and his son, Stone, weren't just any vampires. Stone wasn't even a vampire, or at least not the type that died and rose from the dead. He was a dhampyr, and alive. They'd both given their all to help find my mom, when Merriven had kidnapped her. Upon my return to the security office, I found Dane and the guards already watching the video. "Anything?"

"Not yet." My partner rested his hands on the back of the chair as I sat down." Ernie says it was between two and two-thirty."

"Weirdest thing," the guard said, tapping the mouse. "Here we go."

The camera was in the corner opposite the one Tanisha had said the mirror was in. The video moved as the camera slowly swept side to side. Dane pointed. "There's the mirror."

"This next sweep, look at the bottom of the door," Ernie said. "We didn't notice the first few times through, because we were fast-forwarding."

I had to squint, because the video quality wasn't the best. Something dark curled under the door. There hadn't been any fire damage, and I couldn't remember smelling smoke. "What is that? Smoke?"

"Beats me," Ernie said. "None of the alarms went off."

Several minutes passed; the dark stuff filled the room. Once the camera was picking up nothing but grainy black, the screen flashed white static lines, and then cleared. The room reappeared, and the mirror was simply gone, the dust cloth left crumpled on the floor. Ernie tapped, stopping the video. "See? Weird."

"Yeah. Can we get a copy of it?"

"Sure. It'll take me a few minutes to go grab a disc, oh." He took the USB drive Dane held out. "Handy."

I twisted around to look at my partner. He grinned. "Easier to carry."

"Cool. Did you smell anything in that room?"

"Magic, but it is full of elven artifacts."

Damn, but then again, he'd have mentioned it if he had smelled smoke or something else. I'd learned the only thing that could side-track Dane was a particular brand of ale, and maybe pizza. "We'll take it back to the office. Maybe the boss has seen something like it before."

"Good plan," he agreed.

THREE

Mr. Whitehaven wasn't in the office.

"He was called away," Tabitha said. We'd interrupted her while she was texting, and she kept checking her screen, so it must be a serious conversation keeping her so distracted. "He said he wouldn't be back today."

"Oh."

"Anything I can help with?"

I resisted the urge to grin. It'd taken her long enough to reach the point of trying to get involved in a case. Mr. Whitehaven didn't hire useless people. "I don't know. We have some video you're welcome to take a look at. Maybe you can figure out what it is."

Tabitha's eyes actually sparkled as she set her phone aside, and pushed it out of easy reach. "I'll try."

Dane offered his USB stick, and she quickly plugged it into her computer. We moved around to her side of the desk, and I noticed her phone's screen, or rather, Damien's name on it. So he'd finally begun talking to her. I wondered if he'd asked her out yet while Tabitha started the video.

"Fast forward to about one-fifty-nine AM," Dane said. She did, and we watched the dark stuff. "We don't think it's smoke. Didn't smell anything."

"No, those are shadows.

"Shadows?"

Tabitha nodded, pausing the video. Her short, neatly manicured, sea green-painted nails clicked on the screen as she outlined the darkness. "See how solid the edges are? Smoke or fog would be more diffuse. This is a large concentration of shadows."

Living shadows? "What, or who, can make shadows like this? Or what kind of person is made of shadows?"

She leaned back. "Any type of magic users with the right skills. There are some beings who travel via shadows too, or can control them. There are gods who can manipulate them. I don't know of any species made of shadows though."

Great, a big suspect pool. "That's quite a list. Any chance of narrowing it down?"

"Maybe. Was the door opened?"

"No. No alarms were triggered and these shadows took that. It's the mirror." I pointed to the shrouded shape.

Tabitha hit the play button to watch the rest of the video. "Okay, so nothing physical was interfered with except the mirror, and it wasn't physically carried out."

"Right."

"Not just someone who can control shadows, but someone who can magically transport large objects. Hm." Her eyes narrowed. "I don't think any human magic users could do something like this yet."

"Why not?" I asked.

"It's only been eight years since they gained magic. Shadow magic requires a lot of power and time to learn," she replied. "Most supe species are only able to do limited magic. For example, my people can only change shape and create small magic related to water."

I glanced at Dane, who smiled. "Tab is a Selkie."

"Oh. Cool."

Tabitha giggled. "You don't know what a Selkie is, do you?"

"I know it has something to do with water."

"Yes. We can change from human to seal by putting on our sealskins."

She was a shifter, kind of. Also pretty far from any large bodies of water. "That's pretty nifty. Where do you swim around here? Santo Trueno's not exactly beachfront property."

"There are a few suitable places."

I was being too nosy. "So what kinds of supes can do a lot of magic? I know elves can."

"Aside from them, you're looking at either gods or demons," Dane sighed. "Let's hope it's another elf. I've kind of had enough of gods, and would rather not mess with demons."

That echoed my sentiments exactly. "Elf would be good. Besides, why would a god wait until now to steal the mirror? Wouldn't one be able to nab it whenever?"

Tabitha shrugged. "Guess it would depend on the god. They're notoriously capricious."

Ugh. "I didn't want to hear that."

"Sorry."

"It's okay." I patted her shoulder, and a vision flashed across my mind, of deep green water and furry bodies swimming. It was neat to already know what those furry bodies were. "Thanks."

"You're welcome." She smiled. "I can help a bit more, do some research into gods that are mentioned to have used shadows, if you like?"

"That would be awesome." I checked the time, which was nearly five o' clock. "Please do that, and I think we should pay a visit to Thorandryll."

"Ah, I kind of have a date." Dane straightened up from leaning on Tabitha's desk. "Remember Sheila?"

"Red glasses cutie from the college?"

He nodded. "Yeah. I'm supposed to meet her at six."

"Okay. I can handle talking to Thorandryll myself. Go have fun, and I'll fill you in tomorrow. How about my house around nine in the morning?"

"Sound good, and thanks. Say hello to Kethyrdryll if you see him."

"I will." And hoped I would. Kethyrdryll was the nicest elf I'd met so far, even compared to Alleryn. Thorandryll's brother wasn't an ass to shifters. "See you later."

"Bye, ladies." Dane took off, pulling out his truck keys before he hit the door. I had to grin at his obvious eagerness.

"Do you want me to email the list when I'm done, or print it out?"

"Email's fine, and if you don't mind, send it to us both. But," I gestured at her phone, which had dinged a few times since she'd put it down. "Don't let it interfere with any plans this evening. Thanks again."

"You're welcome."

I waved and left the office, waiting until I was in my car to call ahead. The stereo Logan had put in my car allowed me to use my phone hands-free.

"Miss Jones," Thorandryll answered. "I was just thinking of you."

Sure he was. Then again, with my luck, he probably really had been. "Hello."

"To what do I owe the pleasure of this call?"

"I have a client, an elf, and have some questions you may be able to answer. If you have time."

"Of course. When will you arrive?"

"Maybe a half hour or so from now." Thorandryll's sidhe was on the northeastern-most edge of the city.

"I look forward to seeing you." He ended the call, without saying good-bye.

Hm, maybe I should drive home and teleport from there. It'd give me the chance to feed my dogs. My house lay beyond the north edge of the city, on the west of the highway. Yeah, I'd do that. Wouldn't have to deal with evening traffic that way. Hurray for teleportation, the quickest, greenest way to travel from point A to point B.

FOUR

I teleported to the gates of Thorandryll's sidhe, where two elves stood guard. One was the same elf I'd taken dinner to, when we'd camped in the entrance of the Unseelie castle a couple of weeks before.

He greeted me with a smile and brief inclination of his head. "Welcome, Lady Discord."

"Hi. I'm sorry, I didn't catch your name last time."

"Edrel, my lady."

"Nice to see you again, Edrel. I have an appointment with..."

"The prince, yes. Lord Kethyrdryll will be here momentarily to escort you."

"Cool, thanks." He opened the gate to let me in. The drive wasn't straight, but a thing of curves lined with tall, thick hedges. The better to ambush unwelcome visitors, I guessed. Kethyrdryll came into sight from around the closest curve, and waved. "There he is. Laters."

When I reached Kethyrdryll, he smiled. "It's pleasant to see you again."

"Same here. Are you settling in okay?" Thorandryll's twin had missed the Melding, trapped on his way to visit the Unseelie.

"Well, I think it's all so fascinating, what humans have become, and the things they've created." His smile brightened. "Their story-telling has morphed beyond belief. Television, movies, the Internet...all the new media. That's the correct phrase, isn't it?"

"Yes." I was smiling too; his enthusiasm was amusing. Then again, maybe I took all the conveniences of modern life for granted, having grown up with them.

He glanced back at the gates. "I didn't see a vehicle. Do you have one? I rather like motor vehicles, in spite of their bewildering variety."

"I teleported, but yeah, I have a car. I'll bring it over when I have the chance."

"I plan to learn to operate them in the future."

"Cool." I had to take off my jacket. Thorandryll preferred summer, so it was way warmer inside the sidhe. "It's fun to drive."

We chatted about nothing in particular the rest of the walk, and Kethyrdryll took me inside, straight to his brother's office.

The elven Prince of Santo Trueno sat behind his desk, reading a sheaf of papers. He wore a dark blue poet's shirt, the lacing loose, and if not for his intent frown, he could've graced the cover of a romance novel. His golden hair was long and straight, not a touch of frizz to be seen. Humidity wouldn't dare wreak havoc on an elf's hair.

"Lady Discordia is here," Kethyrdryll said when his brother kept reading.

"Yes, thank you. Please, have a seat."

There was one chair in front of his desk, but this time, I'd called ahead. Which made me wonder if there'd only been the one chair before I called. There'd always been just the right number of chairs on my prior visits, whether with Nick or with Logan and Dane.

I sat, and he kept reading. Two seconds, and boredom set in, along with irritation. A minute later, he was still reading. After debating my options for another minute, I stood up and headed for the door.

"Where are you going?"

"Home. You're obviously busy." I gave myself a point for not sounding huffy.

"My apologies. Please come back."

I turned and he set the papers down, a faint smile on his face. Recalling the time I'd kicked him in the family jewels, I smiled back, probably showing too many teeth, and returned to my seat.

"Before we delve into the matter that brought you here, I must inform you that your debt is due."

"What debt?" What the... "Oh, that. The dinner date for turning me back to normal."

"Yes, I'm hosting a dinner ball on New Year's Eve, and require your presence as my companion for it."

"A dinner ball."

He gave a nod. "Formal dress."

I seriously considered protesting, but I had agreed to the deal, and getting it over with sounded good. "Fine. What time?"

"I'll pick you up at seven."

Ugh, that made it more date than I liked, but hey, I could always teleport home the second we finished eating. "No magic tricks. That was part of the deal."

"No magic tricks," Thorandryll agreed, and changed the subject. "I've been informed you're not seeing anyone."

Instant suspicion. "My dating habits aren't any of your business."

"They are if I plan to request the pleasure of your company in the future.

I shook my head. "Nope. This is a one-time-only deal. You're not my type."

"And why is that, Miss Jones?"

Well, looked like the time for the "Come to Jesus" meeting had arrived, ready or not. "How about a little plain talk? Like the fact I'm twenty-three, which is basically a fetus compared to you."

Thorandryll waved that away with a languid gesture. "Age matters little to my people."

"It matters to me. I have rules about dating: No guys more than two years younger or ten years older. You're a lot more than ten years older."

"What if it would prove highly advantageous for you?"

"I'm not a gold digger, dude. I date somebody because I like him, not because it's 'highly advantageous' to."

He sighed. "I wasn't talking about financial interest, Miss Jones. It would be politically advantageous."

The sound that erupted from me wasn't remotely lady-like, being a snorting laugh. "I have all the politics I can handle right now, so no thanks."

"I don't think you comprehend the state our community's currently in." Thorandryll leaned forward, resting his forearms on his desk. "Things are unsettled."

"Uh-huh, and us dating would make them settle? I find that really hard to believe, but thanks for confirming my suspicion."

Up went his eyebrows. "What suspicion?"

"See, I may be young, but I'm not as dense as you think I am." I smiled. "I knew there wasn't any way you were actually interested in me. Not romantically."

"I do find you attractive. You're a lovely woman."

"Pretty sure you'd be just as interested if I had a face full of hairy moles, because I'm a psychic. Come on." I scowled. "You're an elf prince with loads of gorgeous elf women around."

"And you don't believe I would choose you over any of them?" He tilted his head. "The lack of self-confidence that implies flies into the face of all I know about you."

"I'm self-confident, not stupid. I'm human, I'll age. You won't."

"Debatable," he muttered.

Had I heard him right? "What?"

"Fine, if you don't wish to believe my interest in you is anything beyond," he paused. "I'm not certain how to finish that."

"Greed for power?" I suggested.

He actually rolled his icy blue eyes. "That, I suppose. You don't think very highly of me."

"Gee, wonder why? There's been lies, trouble, oh and you totally took advantage of me while I was having a vision that time, in your library." I hadn't forgotten him macking on me. "I owe you a slap for that, but we'll call it even because I got to kick you."

"Normally, when a woman has the look that you did, she wants to be kissed."

"Vision, jerk. Seriously, who makes with the sexing in a library?" I waved my hand before he could answer. "Doesn't matter. Unless I say 'kiss me', you don't."

Thorandryll raised his eyebrow. "Do you plan to?"

"Hell to the no. I told you, you're not my type. Too old." Too arrogant and conniving, as well.

Thorandryll nodded. "I see. Even though I can give you every luxury imaginable?"

"I'm not really a fan of luxury. Comfortable, now yeah, I like being comfortable. But I don't need a man to make that happen. I can do it myself." I was doing it myself, even though buying the house and adopting five furry kids was costing more than I felt okay with.

"Everyone enjoys a bit of luxury, Miss Jones."

I grinned. "Keyword's a bit. Drowning in it? Not me."

Thorandryll nodded and smiled back. "Very well. Straight talk now, I believe the saying is."

"Okay." Holy crap, had I really convinced him to lay off?

"I am a power in this city. I have a duty to my people, and to those who name Santo Trueno home." He paused, watching my face. "I wish to see this city prosper, and that requires making alliances."

How refreshing was this? He was talking straight.

"As you noted, you are a power in this city as well. A growing power; one that discomfits certain groups."

"Okay."

"It would be beneficial to us both to be allied."

Like I didn't already have enough alliances to keep straight. "In what way?"

"Marriage would be the first option."

I blinked. Did he seriously just...not understand I wanted him to back off? "Option two?"

"Less optimal would be a declared alliance."

I felt my forehead wrinkling. I had declared alliance with the tigers, but was now an adopted clan member. Which meant I was a declared ally of the lions, because the clan was. For all intents, I was an ally of the vampires' Council now too, and possibly the gargoyles as well. "Why is that less optimal?"

"You've chosen allies that aren't acceptable to some of my people. They will wonder where your loyalty truly lies."

Oh, well... "That's easy. People. All the law-abiding and innocent. In fact, make that every living being in Santo Trueno who isn't up to no good."

Thorandryll raised his left eyebrow. "You consider this city yours?"

"I was born here, and have lived here all my life. Yeah, that makes it mine, as much as anyone's." Hell, I'd fought for it against demons, gods, vampires, and dark elves. "I'm not going to marry you to make all the other elves feel better."

"Then you'll agree to a declared alliance?"

"I need to talk to Terra first." I'd done way too much tripping into supe politics in the past year. "Because if I'm your ally, that makes the clan your ally too, and you've made it pretty clear you don't like shifters."

The prince frowned. "Logan has earned a modicum of my respect."

Good to hear, especially since he had a funny way of showing it. "That's nice to know."

"Discuss it with your people and inform me of your decision." He hesitated. "I must request a friendly appearance between us during the ball."

"I'll be nice," I said after swallowing a giggle. "Promise."

"Then let's move onto the matter that brought you here."

"Lady Celadine." Possibly my imagination, but I thought he flinched at her name. "She hired us to find a stolen object, a mirror she loaned to the museum."

"And you require my assistance in what way?"

"She wasn't exactly forthcoming with useful info. I wondered if you could shed any light on why someone might want to steal it."

He smiled, leaning back in his chair. "Anyone able to use magic is interested in acquiring objects of power. How they would use those depends on the object, and I can assure you that the mirror has proven to be remarkably uncooperative to those who have possessed it."

I frowned. "We were told it—he—has an attitude. Do you know how he ended up in the mirror? I mean, he was a person once, right?"

Thorandryll tilted his head to the left. "He was. The legend is that he was a human who angered a god, and thus, was stripped of his body, his soul imprisoned in the mirror."

"That's horrible." I shivered.

"Gods aren't above cruelty, Miss Jones. Hasn't that become clear to you yet?" He stared into my eyes, and I half-expected to have an attack of the hazies, but it didn't happen. "When they walk among us, we would all do well to remember their capacity for cruelty."

"I know. Do you have any idea who the second god was? With Cernunnos?"

Thorandryll shook his head. He hadn't been much help, if I discounted having my worries increased about having gods interested in me. "Okay, thanks."

"Would you stay for dinner?"

"Sorry, can't, but thanks for the offer. Bye." I stood up and teleported home.

With the dogs already fed, I only had my own stomach to worry about. Merriven appeared to watch me build a couple of ham and cheese sandwiches.

"Those look extremely unappetizing."

I ignored him, but he kept yapping while I ate, then followed me into the damn shower. He was still yapping when I finally fell asleep.

FIVE

The insistent blare of my alarm clock opened my eyes and pulled a groan from my throat. With a swing of my arm, I smacked the clock, hitting the snooze button. "Argh."

Leglin chuffed. He hadn't had nightmares about being turned into a vampire by Merriven. I had, and they sucked. The screams and blood were still too vivid, and I discovered dried tears on my face when I rubbed my hand over it.

Roughly twenty minutes later, I was dressed and stretching on my front porch—how awesome was it to be able to say that? My porch?—while the dogs took care of their early morning bladders. Were early-morning jogs really necessary?

Mom had thought it a great idea, but she did yoga four days a week. Like me, she always had several somethings going on at all times, but her time management skills far surpassed mine. Weird, considering I'd tagged along and helped her practically from birth.

I finished stretching, slipped my MP3 player from the pocket of my windbreaker, and stuffed the earbuds into my ears before hitting the play button. "Come on, let's get this over with."

Squishy was the first to meet me at the bottom of the steps, her pink winter coat the only bright spot in the pre-dawn gloom. I shivered while bending to pet her little head. "It's fricking cold."

"*Wuss.*" Bone began walking toward the south side of our property. "*You'll warm up.*"

He was right, but I said, "Remember, slow and easy first."

"*Run, run, run.*" Squishy scurried to Speck, to herd him ahead of her. The black Chihuahua wasn't a fan of my new exercise efforts. He wore a black and red plaid coat, but trembled as though he were freezing to death.

My Pit Crew had laughed at the idea of wearing sweaters or coats. They didn't know I'd ordered them each a hoodie with their names on the backs.

I broke into a slow jog, the bigger dogs ahead, and the two little ones behind. A good PI didn't shirk on exercise the way I had been doing for the past several months. I'd even missed some self-defense classes. Of course, I hadn't exactly been lazy either, with my job being what it was. But a regular fitness regimen? Forget about it.

Nearly everyone I might face would be bigger and stronger. Probably faster too, but that didn't mean I shouldn't try to keep fit. Or that I should grow to rely on my psychic abilities too much, since I knew they weren't always available in some places.

At my slow pace, two songs had played by the time we reached the first back corner of my property. I was already beginning to huff and puff. Slowing to a walk along the back fence, I caught my breath, and couldn't keep from grinning. How cool was it that I'd found such a great place? The dogs spread out, leisurely sniffing the crunchy grass and glistening weeds. It was so cold, the dew had frozen on everything. It was beautiful, and it was all mine.

At the northwest corner, I turned east and began jogging again. Halfway to the front fence, the Chihuahuas began to complain they were tired. I sent them to the house, Diablo going with to make certain they made it.

He caught up with us a couple of minutes later, and at the front northeastern corner, I dropped back to a walk. "Okay, at the driveway, we sprint back to the house."

My legs were feeling the burn, so I wasn't looking forward to the sprint. But hey, at least I wasn't freezing anymore.

The distance from drive entrance to house was longer than I hoped I'd ever have to run from anyone or anything, especially full-out. That's why I was doing it. We reached the asphalt surface too soon for me, but I turned and took off running, trying to convince myself something was chasing me.

Diablo and Bone barked, shooting past. Leglin stayed beside me, adjusting his pace to do it. He wasn't running full out. Didn't have to, to keep up with me.

My heart was pounding triple time, my lungs were burning, and my legs felt ready to fall off. We reached the end of the driveway and I staggered to a stop, gulping air while bending at the waist, my hand pressed to the stitch stabbing me in my side.

More than a few minutes passed before I was able to straighten, and my entire body felt lead-filled. Pacing to cool off, I said, "Whoever said exercise makes you feel great is a raging idiot. I don't feel great. I feel like throwing up."

Diablo snickered from the front porch. "*I feel hungry.*"

"Ugh." Sweat had plastered the tee I wore under the windbreaker to my skin. "Breakfast for you guys. I'm going to take a shower before mine."

The doorbell rang at nine AM, announcing my partner's arrival. When I answered the door, he held up a box of donuts. "They had your favorites."

"You're my bestest friend in the world right now."

Dane grinned. "I have the list Tabitha made too."

"Awesome." We retired to the dinette table—which I really needed to replace for something larger—for coffee and donuts, and to look over the list. He'd brought a work laptop and a few books from his shelves, so we set to work after devouring the donuts. There went my morning's exercise.

A few hours later, Dane sat back and stretched. "I thought I had a decent handle on all the pantheons. I do not. Especially when it comes to the elder gods."

"You're doing better than me. I have no handle at all, and I've met three gods." I stuck a bookmark into the book on Aztec gods I'd been scanning. "Maybe we should take a drive, see if Jo and David can help us out."

"With a lunch stop?"

"No pizza."

"Damn." He stood. "Chinese?"

I nodded. "That'll work. I have to let the dogs out first."

However, we didn't make it to the Blue Orb as planned, because Tanisha from the museum called to let us know she'd located the dust cloth that had covered the mirror. We went there to pick it up after we finished eating.

Once back outside, Dane shook the giant baggie. "Do you want to try it here?"

"Why not?"

I waited for him to open it, and stuck my hand inside. The dust sheet held the remnants of air-conditioning chill. Merriven appeared on top of my car, leaning back to brace his hands, his pale face tilted up to the sun. Frickin' vampire.

Closing my eyes, I opened the doors to two rooms in my mental maze—psychometry and tracking—and waited, reveling a bit in how well I'd managed to follow Sal's suggestion about mental shielding.

We probably looked strange to the few people arriving or leaving the museum. Good thing none of them could see the sunning vampire, who chose to speak. "It won't work. I do believe your powers are waning. What a shame it will be, should you become just another boring human."

Teeth gritted, I concentrated harder. A damn vampiric delusion was not going to shred my self-confidence. After a few more minutes passed, Dane quietly asked, "Anything?"

"Not ye...wait." A thread unfurled, dark gray in color. I'd have to add it to my list, and hope to figure out what the new color stood for. I opened my eyes to find the thread stretching out in mid-air, which was freaky, since it went right through Dane's throat. "I have a trail."

"Yay." He closed the bag while I rushed around to the driver's side. A few seconds later, we were out of the museum parking lot and dodging through traffic. The thread continued to float at eye level, and I wondered if it indicated shadows. The ones involved in the mirror's disappearance had been kind of floaty.

Dane stayed quiet, texting on his phone. I'd never gotten into the habit of texting, but kind of envied him and Tabitha for having someone always there, just a text away.

Not that it was anyone's fault but mine. Logan would probably enjoy seeing texts from me, if I hadn't put him on hold.

We went under an overpass to the west side of Santo Trueno. The city had developed in and around a ravine, spreading out into the gullies cracking either side. The highway ran right through the middle of the ravine's lowest point, splitting the city into unequal halves.

On the west side, the Palisades marked the southernmost end. A few somewhat better neighborhoods spread from there to the north, culminating into a spread of businesses and warehouses. We ended up entering the Heights, in a section roughly center on the west side. I parked in front of a block of offices and shops, across the street from an apartment complex. "It's going between the dry cleaner and that thrift store."

"Okay." Dane had put his phone away when I slowed the car. He climbed out as soon as I turned off the engine, and looked around. "Be nice if we found it sitting in the alley."

"Yes, but don't hold your breath." We began walking.

"I can hold my breath for six minutes."

"I'll add that to my Dane trivia."

He grinned. "My favorite color is orange."

I felt my lips curve. "And your favorite food is pizza, with all the meats and extra cheese."

"Yours is a medium-well steak with a baked potato. Butter, pepper, and sour cream on the potato." We turned down between the two buildings, and he stepped over a damp, flattened cardboard box. "And you don't like to wear jewelry."

"I wear earrings." Our banter actually had a point: We were practicing our observation skills.

"Yes, but only studs. You don't wear rings, bracelets, or necklaces most of the time."

"You prefer tees to shirts with buttons."

Dane looked over at me. "How do you know that? I wear shirts with buttons."

"Yeah, but you constantly fiddle with them when you do. You never tug at your T-shirts." I stopped, because we'd reached the alley. "Well, that was helpful."

"What?"

"The thread ends right there." I pointed to the air in front of us. "Just beyond the edges of the buildings."

"No mirror in sight." Dane walked into the alley to look around. I stayed put, studying the ground below and air above the thread's end point. Merriven slid into my peripheral vision, whispering endearments, and then insults as I ignored him.

I wished he were solid so I could set his aggravating ass on fire, especially when he shoved his fist through my chest, baring his fangs right in my face.

Dane returned from checking both directions. "Nothing."

My phone beeped, indicating its battery was low. We turned to walk back to my car. "Well, that was a waste of time. Guess we should head to the shop to talk to David and Jo now." After that, I needed to take care of my dogs, and had that appointment with Lord Derrick about my Merriven problem.

Dane had a field day, looking through my MP3 collection as we drove to the Blue Orb. "You listen to country?"

"Sometimes. Don't judge."

"I'm totally judging, because...oh my God, Cordi. Nickelback? Really?"

"Hey." I smacked his fingers away from the stereo. "No judging. I've heard you humming 'MMMBop' more than a few times."

"At least it's not by Nickelback."

"I like Nickelback, so shut up."

He snorted. "Your taste in music? It leaves a lot to be desired."

"Says Mr. I Listen to Boy Bands."

"You're just jealous my taste in music exceeds yours. I know good music."

I laughed. "You don't listen to anything more than four years old, unless you're in someone else's car. You don't know the tip of Mount Good Music."

"Yeah? Prove you do."

"Find 'Bohemian Rhapsody' on there and start it."

Dane tried to resist, but failed, when the head banging part began.

We pulled up at the shop, and sat in my car to finish our over-dramatic, lip-syncing second run through of "Bohemian Rhapsody" before heading into the shop.

I loved the Blue Orb. The combination of herbs, scented candles, and incense made walking in feel as though I'd entered a different world. When I had the time, I enjoyed browsing around to see what unknown things I might find.

Today, it was busy. I waved at Jo, who was running the cash register, and then at Tonya as she went past with a customer in tow. David was helping an intense-looking, thin young woman select a crystal. I could hear a few voices from some of the aisles we couldn't see down.

With a few minutes of down time, I decided to tease my partner. "How'd your date go?"

Dane grinned. "Sheila's really smart, and we had fun."

"Was there kissing?"

"Nosy."

"Just returning the favor."

"She let me kiss her good night. There was hand holding."

"Ooh, Dane and Sheila sitting in a tree," I had to stop to keep from laughing, ducking away from his attempts to muss my hair. "Quit it."

"Children, behave," Jo called from the register. We walked to the counter, ignoring her reprimand, jostling and smacking at each other's hands as he kept trying to mess with my hair.

Jo's short auburn hair bounced when she shook her head. "You two are in good moods. What's up?"

"We need some, stop it," I smacked Dane in the stomach to make him lower his arms. "Help with research."

My partner stopped trying to mess up my hair, and slung his arm around my shoulders. "Shadow manipulation that can move solid objects."

Jo blinked. "Well, there's one I haven't heard."

Looked like Tabitha was right. I glanced at Dane, who continued. "We're thinking either elf, god, or demon, and want to try and narrow it down."

She looked at me. "Do you ever have normal cases anymore?"

"Sorry."

"Okay." Jo huffed air out, her hazel eyes glazing over. "Right off-hand, I doubt we'll be able to give you any elf names."

I nudged Dane with my elbow. He dug out the list we'd printed from his back pocket. "Tabitha gave us a starting point."

She took the list when he held it out, scanned it, and shook her head. "This is a good start, but I'd think any god could manipulate shadows if he or she wanted to. So trying to pinpoint a particular one could result in bupkis."

"Great." I sighed. "Guess we'll have to play it by ear then."

"Hit up Prince Snooty for elf names," she said. "If it's demons..."

"We'll ask the boss to loan us his sharp, shiny demon-killing blades," I finished. "Okay."

"We'll look through these names though, just in case, and see if there's any other possibilities." Jo smiled. "What's the missing object?"

"You won't believe this. It's the mirror from Snow White."

She scrunched her face. "I wouldn't think it was a big deal. Didn't it speak riddles and compliment the vanity of the Evil Queen?"

"Yeah, I think that's what it did. Apparently the real mirror is perv who likes to make sexual comments."

Jo laughed. "Figures. Well, I'll let you know if we come up with anything."

"Thanks." When Dane dropped his arm from my shoulders, I leaned over the counter to give her a hug. "Talk to you later."

"Bye."

Once back in the car, we looked at each other. I shrugged. "Well, now what?"

"Nothing new on the Psychic Hotline?"

"Nope."

He drummed his fingers on his thigh. "No leads to follow at the moment. No way of determining who or what the thief is. Sounds like we're at a dead end right now, unless you want to go talk to Thorandryll."

I started my car. "Let's call ahead."

The elf who answered the phone apologized, but said Thorandryll was busy. "I'm afraid the final preparations for the ball are consuming everyone's time and attention right now."

"Okay. Please tell him I called."

"Of course, Miss Jones." The elf, who hadn't given her name, ended the call. We looked at each other again, and this time, Dane shrugged.

"Feel like helping me pick out flowers? I'm going out with Sheila again tonight."

It wasn't even three yet, and my appointment with Derrick was at seven. "Sure."

SIX

After flower shopping, I headed home to do some housework and take care of the dogs. That kept me busy until it was time to teleport to the Barrows, or more specifically, Lord Derrick's front door.

No guards were on duty there, but Stone answered my knock. "Come in."

He led me to the dining room, and pulled out the chair on Derrick's right for me. There were only the three places set, waiting for the meal to be served. I wondered if Derrick had one to be polite, or for another reason.

Once seated, I didn't know how to explain why I was there. Derrick and Stone simply waited until I asked, "Do vampires have a tendency to become ghosts when they die?"

"A tendency? No, it's rare, and in the few cases I'm aware of, the vampires who did become ghosts were less than a decade into their second lives." Derrick's lips turned down in a brief frown. "Are you here because of your late friend?"

"Kind of."

"If she weren't at peace, she was young enough to become a ghost, but I don't sense any dead lingering near you."

I stared at him. Lord Derrick had been turned young—well, young for modern times—and looked around twenty, with shoulder-length, light brown curls, and a rather pretty, unlined face. He'd told me he had three psychic abilities. Was this a second one? "You can sense ghosts?"

"Vampires are closer to the dead than any other species is," Stone said in his deep, gravelly voice.

"Oh. That's pretty sucky. Can you sense ghosts?" Maybe it was a vampire thing then, not a psychic ability. Stone was alive, able to eat food and walk in the sunlight, though he also needed blood. I wasn't sure of all the differences between vampires and dhampyrs. Asking questions to fill in the blanks was a habit I intended to build. The huge man shook his head in answer. I looked back at his father. "Can you sense a ghost even if it's not here right now?"

"Yes. Ghosts leave a residue," he waved his hand. "A psychic odor, if you will. I don't detect that odor on you."

"Okay, so neither of them is a ghost." Then what the hell were they? Delusions as I'd first decided?

"Neither of them, who?" Both men were watching me.

"Wait, you said Ginger could've come back as a ghost."

"If she weren't at peace, yes."

"But you don't smell ghost on me. Does it wear off fast?" A tiny flicker of hope had kindled in me.

"No, the residue clings for months."

I sagged back in my chair, a huge smile nearly splitting my face in two. "Then he lied."

Ginger, the real one, hadn't come back as a ghost. Surely she would've, if I had accidentally murdered her because of Merriven. Okay, I had still killed her, but because she really, truly wanted out, not because of him. Eyes closing, I basked in the deep, hot wave of relief that filled me from toes to head. "Thank God."

"Miss Jones?"

"Cordi." I opened my eyes, grinning at them. "You guys can call me Cordi." Anyone who lightened my huge burden of guilt absolutely deserved the title of friend, as far as I was concerned. "Thank you for telling me that."

"You're welcome. May I ask why that information helped?" Derrick tilted his head.

"Merriven told me he made Ginger ask me to stake her. Told me she didn't really want to die."

"Ah." The vampire nodded. "I see. A terrible burden to place upon someone. In the future, remember that it's difficult for us to force another vampire to ask for the final death. We will only ask if that is truly what we desire."

Nodding, I felt my smile fading. "That helped a lot, but it doesn't actually solve my problem."

"Which is?"

"I have nightmares. I'm pretty used to them, because I've been having them since my psychometry ability kicked in. After he told, I mean, lied to me about Ginger, I was having nightmares about her nearly every night." I paused for breath. "Then I began seeing her when I was awake."

"Now you know she's not a ghost," Derrick said.

"Yeah, but she, or whatever was pretending to be her, is gone. I haven't seen her since we got back from the Unseelie realm."

"You're seeing someone else," Stone said, and I nodded. "Who?"

"Merriven."

Derrick frowned. "He was too old to return as a ghost."

"Right. I started seeing him five days ago. He walked straight out of the tigers' Solstice bonfire and has been hanging around since. Only he talks to me. Ginger never did, not while I was awake."

The two men traded a look before Derrick spoke. "Escalation."

"Huh?"

"The first illusion didn't speak. The second does, which is an escalation."

"Oh. Yeah." Duh. It was a logical observation. "But what are they? I thought maybe I was having delusions because of guilt, but I don't feel a damn bit guilty over Merriven."

Derrick chuckled. "No reason for you to. These illusions are obviously meant to affect you negatively, which means someone wishes to harm you. Who would gain from doing so?"

Good question. The only answer I could come up with was, "Maybe a vampire?"

"I don't know of any able to create illusions another can see without there being blood exchanged." Derrick shook his head, his brow furrowing.

"Elves are masters of illusion," his son remarked, as the dining room door opened. Servants entered, and speedily emptied the trays they carried. We waited until they left before picking up the conversation again.

Derrick had a bowl of pale, pink broth. It smelled like chicken and copper. I chose not to comment on it. "The only elf I know I've pissed off is the prince. I don't think I've done it enough to make him decide to drive me bonkers."

"The gods often drove people mad with illusions." Derrick dipped a spoon into his bowl. I picked up my fork and tried a bite of the linguini on my plate. It was delicious.

"I kind of met someone that happened to. A psychic."

"Rhaetha."

I huffed. "How do you find this stuff out?"

Derrick smiled. "The Unseelie's reappearance was a rather big event. I'd heard of her, and knew the Unseelie had captured her. Bits of gossip have been floating about, Miss Cordi."

My head bowed. "So you know what happened."

"That you saved Queen Maeve's life? Yes."

My next bite tasted like ashes. "Rhaetha was a psychic. Like me. But she was victimized by Morpheus and Maeve, and I killed her."

"True, but I assure you, it's better for the world that Rhaetha is dead. She would've laid waste with her every step, and killed everyone who crossed her path."

He was probably right, but that didn't make me feel any better about it. "I guess."

"You ended centuries upon centuries of misery for her," Derrick quietly said.

By frying her with electrokinesis. Cooking her from the inside out. I shuddered and put my fork down, my appetite gone. "Can we go back to my immediate problem, please?"

"Certainly. Elves, gods, and there's always the possibility someone has cursed you."

"The only curser I know who had a problem with me is dead." Dalsarin had turned me into a dog, which had been pretty interesting and was the reason I could now talk to dogs.

Stone swallowed his last bit of linguini. "Crossed any witches lately?"

"Nope." The only witches I knew were friends. "Who else can do curses?"

"Anyone with magical ability and no issues hurting others."

I scowled at my plate. "I'm pretty sure I haven't pissed off anyone but vampires and Thorandryll."

"You killed Apep's Avatar, and were involved in bringing about the death of Morpheus." Derrick focused on his broth when I transferred my scowl from my plate to him.

"Thanks for reminding me." Crap, it certainly appeared a god was the logical choice. I sighed. "How do I find out which one is behind it?"

"Ask. Perhaps Cernunnos or the other god who took part in ending Morpheus knows."

"I'm really beginning to feel like people know more about my life than I do." My complaint earned quick grins from both of them. "It's not funny."

"Of course not," Derrick agreed before putting his spoon aside and lifting a snowy, linen napkin to dab his lips. "But it is something you'll grow accustomed to."

"People being nosy? I doubt it." Being a private investigator, I was supposed to be the nosy one.

"You're a person of interest to many, even beyond Santo Trueno. It's been quite some time since a psychic with many abilities has walked among us. You're dangerous now, even as young and relatively inexperienced as you are. They'll watch and listen as you grow into your full potential." Derrick's expression was solemn.

A chill chased the length of my spine. "What if some of them don't like what they hear or see?"

"You don't need us to tell you," Stone said. "You already know the answer."

Yeah, I did. Either someone would try to kill me, or I'd end up in the Unseelie dungeon, under lock and key. I felt my bottom lip quiver and forced it to stop by pressing my lips together. "Being a psychic really sucks ground glass sometimes."

"Colorful sentiment." Derrick smiled, a sympathetic glint crossing his face. "My advice is to continue what you're doing, and make this city fully yours."

I started, my eyes widening. "I'm not..."

"But you are. You've allied yourself with a powerful coven. You are in the employ of a powerful and highly respected lord. My people are in your debt, and you are a queen of the city's tiger clan." He rested his elbows on the arms of his chair, clasping his hands together across his stomach. "Through your clan, you are also allied with the Pride. The Lord of the Hunt has an interest in you, as well as that other god. The Unseelie owe you twice over, for helping to free them and for saving their Queen, and you have friends among the Seelie."

I tried to protest again. "I didn't mean to do any of that stuff."

The vampire laughed. "No, and that makes it all the more frightening. You didn't plan any of it. You simply try to help people, and these are the results. You're a wild card, unpredictable in the extreme."

Maybe I needed to rethink my decision to keep my job. Early retirement certainly looked super-attractive about then. If it weren't for the fact I had a pack to feed and a thirty-year mortgage hanging over my head, I could retire and move to some quiet, little corner of the country after bleaching my hair and having a bit of plastic surgery. I'd need to change my name too. "Why me?"

Stone snorted while taking a drink, and choked. Tea splattered down his chin and dotted his dark blue shirt. He caught his breath, laughed, and cleared his throat. "You're just lucky that way."

My glare earned another deep laugh from him. "Doesn't feel like luck. More like I have the Doom of Damocles hanging over me."

"Rest assured that I will inform you, should I learn of any viable threats," Derrick said. "And I swear upon my blood that I will stand with you against them."

I blinked and felt odd for a few seconds, surprised. Sure, we were definitely on friendly terms now, but promising to fight on my behalf, like some knight of old? "Wouldn't that make you a target?"

"Yes."

"Then don't say that."

"It's already said."

"Look, I apparently have a pissed-off god on my butt. I don't want anyone dying because of me." Unless they deserved it, I silently amended. Once, I would've thought he did just because he was a vampire, but not anymore. Strange as it was to think, Derrick and Stone were good people.

Derrick inclined his head. "Your concern for my well-being is a welcome change, and I thank you for it, but I've made my choice."

Freakin' stubborn vampire. I glanced across the table at Stone, hoping he'd say something. He did, but not what I silently urged him to. "My master speaks for me as well."

Damn it. I'd only come here for information, and had face-planted into a pair of declared allies. Hadn't Patrick, Nick's aggravating older brother, said something about Fate? Yeah, he'd called her an old hag. I agreed with his assessment and wondered if there were anything I could say to change their minds. Nothing popped up so I gave in to the inevitable. "Thank you."

"If it helps, we both have several centuries of survival practice." Derrick grinned.

I had to grin back. "Yes, that does help."

I needed time to digest things, so decided to walk to my favored exit from the Barrows before teleporting home. My path led me past the late Lady Esme's estate.

The gates were opened, and it didn't look as though anyone had moved in. I stopped and checked the top of the walls on either side, wondering why. Gargoyles perched along them at irregular intervals. Maybe it was theirs now? Focusing on the one at the left of the gate, I said, "Hello."

Gray stone turned to red scales, and the gargoyle tilted its parrot-beaked snout down to look at me. I hadn't actually expected a response. "Hi. I'm..."

"Lady Discordia Jones," the gargoyle rasped. "We know you."

"Oh, cool. I was just," I stopped, because it probably had seen me walk up. "Just wondering how Tase is."

Parrot Beak stared at me. I heard the weird grinding in my head, which seemed to be the sign of telepathic communication among gargoyles. "Step inside."

"Okay." I took a few steps forward, and halted, checking over my shoulder. "Is this..."

Something landed on my head, whipping the back of my hair into a frenzied cloud. A small, feline head slid into view from above. My eyes crossed when I tried to focus upward. "Hi, Tase."

The tiny gargoyle's tail kept wagging, and he patted the bridge of my nose with his miniature hand. "I knew you'd come back to see me."

My eyes felt strained, but I smiled, wondering when he'd become so talkative. I'd been lucky to get two words, via telepathy at that, from him the first time we met. "You're too cute to forget." I lifted my hand. "Would it be okay if you sat here instead of on my head?"

His response was a leap and turn. Tase sat up, his tail winding over the edge of my hand to anchor himself. I melted when he smiled at me, baring his itty bitty fangs and wrinkling his short snout. Baby gargoyles were precious. Or at least Tase was. "What have you been up to?"

He straightened to his full height, which was roughly six inches. "I am learning to read."

"Wow. That's awesome." I wondered why a gargoyle would need that skill, but didn't ask because he was smiling again.

Tase stretched out his puny wings. "And I am learning how to use my magic. Mama says it's time for that."

"You're a busy boy." Movement on the right caught my attention. Merriven wiggled his fingers in greeting. Tase turned his head and froze. A second later, his terrified squeal rang in my ears as the baby gargoyle lunged from my hand to bury himself in my hair.

"Oh, crap," I muttered as every gargoyle in sight suddenly became animated, and back-pedaled when a large, dark figure landed with a thump in front of me. "I didn't hurt him."

Petra, Tase's mother, hissed while settling back on her haunches. The other gargoyles returned to stone. Realizing my hands were raised in a "Stop" gesture, I lowered them. "Sorry."

Then the little gargoyle's reaction hit me like a sledgehammer. Tase had seen Merriven. A sideways flick of my eyes confirmed the vampire, or rather, illusion of him, was still present. "Wait a minute. Can you see him?"

Petra turned her head to follow my forefinger as I stabbed it in Merriven's direction. "I see nothing."

Damn it, I'd hoped she could, that it was some gargoyle super-vision or something. Tase shivered, slipping from my hair to my shoulder. I felt him push his head forward while sliding his tail around the back of my neck. "It's him, Mama. The one who killed our lady and her family."

Verbal confirmation the little guy could see Merriven wasn't necessary by that point. I felt awful he was scared, but slightly relieved, too. "I'm sorry. I had no idea this would happen."

Petra growled, still inspecting the spot Merriven stood. "You see that foul creature?"

"Unfortunately, yes." I held absolutely still when she swung her head my way. Warm breath, redolent of cinnamon, gusted over my face before Petra drew in a deep breath.

"You've been hexed."

Hexed, the same thing as cursed—or I thought they meant the same thing. "Looks that way."

"Come." She turned while rising to all fours, and I ducked to avoid the lash of her spade-tipped tail. Petra prowled away, her massive, lion's mane-embellished head lowered. Tase tucked his head against my ear to say, "Mama can fix it. I haven't learned how to yet."

"Really?" Without waiting for his answer, I hurried after her.

"Yes. Mama knows so much. I'll never learn it all."

I reached up to gently pat the side of his small body. "I bet you will. Little ones learn things faster than big people do."

"We do?"

"Yep. My mom says babies and little kids are like sponges. They soak up everything."

"What's a sponge?" Tase wanted to know.

"Tell you what, the next time I have to come down here, I'll bring one," I promised. "So you can see how they work for yourself."

Petra led us around the dark pile of rocks passing for a vampire mansion, and to a smaller pile that formed a cave. "Wait here."

"Yes, ma'am." She disappeared into the opening, while I sat down on a convenient rock. Tase's breath, also fragrant with cinnamon, tickled my earlobe as he sniffed. "What are you doing?"

"Trying to smell the hex."

"Oh." I closed one eye, forcing myself not to flinch when his tiny, cold nose touched down behind my ear. "Okay."

A few more sniffs, and he stopped. "I found it. It smells like mold."

Lovely. "How did you pick it out?"

"I remember how you smelled before, and searched for a difference." He sneezed, a wee "Ah-ah-choo!" and I fought a giggle. "You smell more like tigers now, too."

"They adopted me into their clan."

"Neat." He leaned against my neck. "Is he still there?"

"Yes." I could see Merriven from the corner of my eye. The vampire, or illusion of him, was preoccupied with studying a statue. He didn't appear to be worried, and that made me worry. Maybe Petra wouldn't be able to fix things.

The thought summoned her from the cave, something dangling from her mouth. Padding over, she sat down, and removed the item. A clear, golden-hued stone hung from a brown leather thong. I leaned forward for a closer look, and saw a drop of dark red suspended in the middle of the tear-shaped stone, which was attached to the thong by a nearly translucent net of delicate wires.

"My son is not yet old enough to uphold his responsibilities to you."

"What? Tase isn't..."

"He chose you. As I am free, I will stand in his place until he's ready."

I remembered Damian telling me to talk to David about gargoyles, and regretted having forgotten to do so while there earlier. "I don't understand."

"Our race was created to be guardians. My son chose you." Petra's wings rustled. She held out the necklace. "This will negate the hex until you discover the being responsible. When you do, call my son's name. I will come, and deal with the matter."

"Deal" sounded a lot like "kill" to me, but being on unexpected ground indicated caution was necessary. "Thank you."

"Put it on, so he goes away," Tase said. "Thank you, mama."

I obeyed the little guy, pretty eager to see the last of Merriven myself. Watching the vamp, who'd suddenly become interested in what we were doing, I pulled the leather thong over my head. As it passed eye-level, the vampire disappeared. "I can't see him anymore. Can you, Tase?"

He moved, sticking his head out to look under my chin. "No. I told you Mama would fix it."

"Do not remove it," Petra said.

"Will water hurt it?"

"No."

No need to skip bathing then. "Thank you so much."

"You will thank me by visiting regularly."

I noted the tips of her fangs and nodded. "Yes, ma'am. I can do that. How often should I visit?"

"He is your guardian, or will be. Until he is able to attend to his duties, you will visit weekly. The bond between you must be allowed to strengthen." She tilted her massive head ever-so-slightly. "I had expected you would come sooner."

Fan-freaking-tastic. I'd definitely tripped into another unplanned alliance, just by poking around a murder scene. Tase purred, the soft sound faint comfort as he snuggled against my neck. Why on earth had the cute little guy chosen me?

"I'm sorry. I'm going to need a bit more information, because I don't know anything about gargoyles, and I don't really understand what you mean when you say he chose me."

Petra lowered her front half, to sit like a cat. "He shouldn't have chosen anyone until his second decade."

Dollars to donuts, his doing so was probably my fault. "Oh."

"The more time spent together, the stronger the bond between you." She paused. "He will be with you until your last breath, a personal guardian against any who choose to attack you by magic or physical means."

I gulped. That was a heavy commitment for someone who'd freaked out over a thirty-year mortgage, and wasn't sure she was ready for a long-term boyfriend. Especially since the newest commitment was in the form of small, fragile, baby creature. One with a really frightening, huge mother. Right then and there, I vowed to talk to David as soon as possible. "I understand. I'll be here every week."

She nodded her massive head, apparently satisfied. "I begin to glean the reasons for his choice."

I didn't, but now knew why she'd been so easy to convince, when I'd come to her for help in defeating Merriven when he'd kidnapped my mother.

"He will tell me if you call for him. Do so as needed. I will come."

Which would surprise the hell out of anyone after me. Having a secret weapon like her might prove super-useful. "Thank you again, and I'm sorry this happened."

"He chose you. A gargoyle's choice is seldom a matter for regret."

SEVEN

After spending about an hour chatting with Tase, who'd quickly begun to remind me of my little brothers, I teleported home to a cacophony of barking. "Come on, guys."

"*Door, door, door,*" Squishy yapped, running in circles around the dining table. It was becoming more obvious, day by day, that the pudgy little Chihuahua wasn't quite right in the head. I couldn't blame her, after what she'd been through. She was one of the little dogs we'd rescued from the dog fighters. She was sweet when she wasn't bossing Speck around, but she was funny when she was harassing him, too. My "Enough barking!" shut the noise down. Speck uttered one more soft yip. His little barker occasionally got stuck.

Bright eyes, wagging tails, and wide doggy grins greeted me as I joined the big dogs at the door. With them there, I didn't bother looking through the peephole before unlocking and opening the door.

Logan staggered, trying to keep his balance as Leglin, Bone, and Diablo rushed out and across the porch, Speck prancing in their wake. "Hi."

"Hi. Hang on." I left to catch Squishy, who was still running laps. "Time to potty."

She wiggled, licking my chin when I tucked her against my chest for carrying. Logan leaned against the porch railing, his hands in his pockets, and watched me put Squishy down. I winced when she overshot the first step and face-planted on the third. Squishy regained her feet, shook off the fail, and scampered away. "*Potty, potty, potty.*"

With a shake of my head, I looked at Logan. "What's up?"

"Not much. Your car's about due for an oil change."

I leaned against the wall beside the front door, and crossed my arms. "You didn't have to walk over to remind me."

He scanned my face before his cute grin made an appearance. "I know."

"I kind of skipped dinner. Any chance you're hungry?" I let my arms fall, smiling back at him. It was hard not to smile. He was one of the coolest people I knew, and that particular grin was totally adorable. We liked each other, enough that I had a dating rain check in my pocket. And we'd snuggled a few times in the not-too-distant past.

"A snack would be nice."

"You can have a snack. I'm going to pig out." I waved my hand toward the dark front yard. "Once everyone's finished."

"I'll watch them, if you want to go ahead."

My stomach was softly protesting the paltry amount of linguini I'd given it. "Okay, gonna take you up on that offer. I'll be in the kitchen."

"See you in a few."

More like a half hour, I thought, walking into the house and shutting the door. Speck was finicky about pottying. My black, thin-legged Chihuahua always had to find just the right spot to do his business. Fortunately, Diablo had taken to the little fella, and always kept an eye on him. Speck sometimes wandered a full acre before finding his perfect potty spot, which meant keeping an eye out while jogging. I'd stepped in one of his "special" potty spots that morning.

In the kitchen, I poked around in the fridge and pantry before deciding more pasta was the right choice.

The front door opened and closed twice, as Logan let in Bone, and then Leglin shepherding Squishy, back in. I cut smoked ham into bite-sized chunks while pasta shells simmered and a slab of sharp cheddar melted.

By the time I had those three ingredients mixed and was sliding the baking dish into the oven, the front door opened again. Logan followed Diablo and Speck inside. "All accounted for."

"Thanks. Dinner will be ready in ten. Do you want beer, tea, or wine?"

"Whatever you're having is fine." He crossed to the breakfast bar and climbed onto a stool. "Smells good."

"Mac and cheese with ham." I poured two glasses of a fruity white, and passed him one.

"Thank you. How are things?"

I took a sip before answering. "Better than they were. Mostly."

"Good."

Turning away, I collected bowls and spoons. "You didn't come over here just to remind me about an oil change."

"No, I came because I wanted to see you. Haven't since Solstice night."

One of the things I liked about him: Once he decided on something, he didn't backtrack or beat around the bush on anything pertaining to it. "Yeah, I've been busy. Holidays and family stuff."

"How 'mostly' better are things?"

I picked up my wineglass and nearly shrugged. Catching myself in time, I answered the question. "I found out what Merriven said was a big, fat lie. That helped a lot, but then I found out someone hexed me, which is why I was seeing things. That, I didn't mention to you, but I was seeing Ginger, then Merriven. While I was awake."

Logan's brows drew together, and his voice was slightly deeper when he asked, "Who hexed you?"

"I don't know yet, just relieved I'm not going crazy. But," I fished the stone out of under the neck of my shirt by its thong. "This is blocking the hex."

His eyes widened. "Where the hell did you find a Gargoyle's Tear?"

"Funny story. I seem to have been adopted by a baby gargoyle."

"Tase."

I nodded. "Yep. His mother gave me this. She decided to stand in for him until he's old enough to start being my guardian. Whatever that actually means. I mean, I have an..." the oven timer dinged. "Just a minute."

About five minutes passed before I was seated next to him, full bowls of gooey deliciousness in front of us. Stealthy paw steps heralded the appearance of my three big dogs. "You guys had your dinner. This is ours."

"So Petra's acting as your guardian. That's good. I thought you seemed less jumpy when you answered the door."

I grimaced. "Crap. I've been trying to act normal."

Logan smiled. "You did a pretty good job. But sometimes, you'd look at something and kind of flinch. Now I know why."

"Sorry I didn't share then. I was really convinced I was on my way to Happyville Manor."

"You don't owe me an apology for wanting to keep something private. The only help I could have offered would have been suggesting you talk to Moira about it."

Which reminded me... "I think I still need to talk to her about something else."

"I can call her over here," he offered. "And leave so you two can talk."

Wow, Nick wouldn't have offered to take a powder. He would've wanted to be right in the middle of it. "Thanks, but not right now. I don't think it's life- or brain-threatening. It's about that dream, when we were in the Unseelie realm."

"The one you were a White Queen in, or the one we talked to Sal in?"

"First. Because." I hesitated. "I saw the ancestors on Solstice Night, and there was an empty place where that White Queen was supposed to be."

"That's definitely Moira's territory," he said. "I've never seen the ancestors."

"You haven't?"

Logan shook his head. "Nope. Not enough mysticism in me. I'm too grounded in the here and now."

"Discord Jones, natural mystic?" I made a face. "That sounds kind of dumb. I don't usually see ... oh, I guess I do see things. But those are because of my abilities, not woowoo visions of spirits."

He laughed. "Except you've seen the ancestors three times, two when you were awake. And I don't think I was dreaming the other time.

"Hallucination?"

"I hallucinated the exact same thing you dreamed?"

"Well, when you put it that way." I took a drink of my wine. "How did you know it was me?"

"The same way I know who's who when we've all shifted." Logan's smile returned. "I could see you looking out."

Confused, I had another drink. "See me?"

"Maybe 'sense' is a better word."

That felt more logical. Sort of. "Anyway, I'm wondering what happened to her, and hoping Moira could tell me."

"Are you sure you don't want to talk to her tonight?"

I glanced at the clock on my stove top. It was after ten. "No, that's okay. It's kind of late."

"Okay, but I doubt she'd mind."

"Kind of need to figure out who cursed me, and we have a case, oh, and Thorandryll called in my debt."

Logan frowned. "Let me guess: His New Year's Eve ball."

"Yeah. How did ..."

"We received invitations to it this afternoon. Our queen plus three."

I snorted. "Wait. Prince Snooty Pants sent invitations to his big important bash to people he can't stand?"

"I was wondering why, but now I know. It's because of you. You're a queen of our clan, and elves have rules about proper protocol. Leaving a queen without the support of her people is," he made air quotes, "Not done."

"Elves are weird."

"Yes, they are."

"Don't torture yourselves on my account," I said. "Though it would be Terra's first public appearance as official Queen. Right?"

"Right."

"Which isn't a bad thing. Is it?"

Logan agreed it wasn't, before saying, "It's not as though I'm in charge anymore. Terra wants to go. She'll want to more once she knows you'll be there too."

"Should I apologize?"

He grinned. "No. I like it when the people I care about care about each other too."

"Makes life easier, huh?" Personally, I liked knowing I was one of the people he cared about. I took a bite before saying, "Anything you can tell me about gargoyles would really help."

"What do you know so far?"

"Not much other than they're guardians, and choose who they'll be that for. Petra told me Tase shouldn't have picked anyone yet.

He's too young. I have to go see him every week, to strengthen our bond."

"Okay. They can't help you during the day unless you're on the verge of death. But at night, there's practically nowhere you can go that they can't. They're proficient magic users, skilled in warding, healing, and charms for all occasions." Logan gestured at the Tear then his bowl. "This is good."

"Thanks."

"Gargoyles are feared warriors. It's nearly impossible to kill one, because they can turn from stone to flesh at will, at least at night. Even if you get a lucky stab in, no guarantee you'll hit anything important." He touched his chest. "Their insides move around."

I swallowed a bite. "That's kind of gross."

Logan grinned. "But useful."

He had a point. Hard to stab something in the heart if it could move that organ out of the way. Or keep it tucked behind less important organs.

"Their loyalty is legendary. They'll take on anyone and anything."

"Okay, so what's the catch?"

Logan chuckled. "You've never seen a gargoyle eat. Might want to think about fencing a few acres in and buying some cattle."

"*Mm, steak on the hoof,*" Bone said from by my feet.

"Discord Jones, future small rancher." I was going to go bankrupt. "I'll be in the poorhouse in less than ten years."

"You're clan. Anyone you're beholden to, we are."

I savored another bite, enjoying the blend of sharp, melty cheese and smoky meat. "You guys aren't responsible for my debts or the crazy situations I get myself into."

"Cordi, we're clan. You have access to whatever we have. Open checkbook. You made having our own sanctuary a reality."

Yes, I'd had a hand in that, but... "I'll figure it out."

"You don't have to. You've made a lifetime's worth of contributions to the clan already. You're in good standing for oh, about a thousand years." Logan smiled.

I laughed. "You did all the hard work. I only twisted Thorandryll's arm a little bit."

"We'll handle the cattle when the time comes. And whatever he's big enough to eat when Tase comes to live with you."

"Live with me?"

"Of course."

There went my sole guest room. "Okay. Right. Of course he'll live here."

Logan finished his wine. "Mind if I ask a question?"

"Shoot."

"Now that you've solved part of the problem, and know what the other part is, are you going to cash in that rain check?"

"I don't know. How do you feel about dating a cursed woman?"

His cute, boyish grin reappeared. "Does 'I'll take you anyway I can get you' make me sound desperate?"

My brain wouldn't let the "I'll take you" pass without tossing up some suggestions on the subject. Heat began to spread up from my throat, and I hoped my face didn't turn bright red. "Desperate, no. Tired of being put on hold, yes. And I'm really sorry about that. I just didn't..."

Logan put his hand on my knee. "No apology necessary. You had something going on. Still do, so if I'm being pushy here, say so. If I'm not, how about dinner tomorrow night?"

"Dinner sounds great, but I may have to postpone if something comes up on the case we have."

He nodded. "I know that's a possibility."

I kind of wanted to yell "Wheeee!" but managed to keep from sounding like a complete idiot. "Okay, we're on for dinner tomorrow night. What time?"

"Seven?"

"Yes. Meet or?" His hand was still resting on my knee, the warmth of it penetrating my jeans.

"You can pick me up here, unless something happens and it's better to meet."

"Okay, cool." I hoped my smile didn't make me look stupid. It felt like it'd taken over my entire face. Looking at our bowls, I realized we'd both finished eating. "Feel like a cup of coffee?"

"Thanks for helping with the cleanup."

"Thanks for feeding me." He finished his coffee and rinsed the cup before placing it in the dishwasher. "I should get out of here so you can go to bed."

Slightly disappointed he was leaving, I nodded. "Okay, I'll walk you out."

"Oh, wait," I said when we reached the door. "I owe the girls a shopping trip, and sleepover. Belated Christmas gifts."

"Terra will understand you're busy."

I rolled my eyes. "Silly man, no woman's too busy for shopping. Besides, I need a dress for the party. Doesn't Terra?"

His expression twisted. "Damn, it is fancy dress. I'm going to have to wear a monkey suit."

Laughter escaped me. "Sorry. Yep, you'll have to get a tux."

"Yes, she'll need a dress."

"Great. I'll call tomorrow, and we'll plan it for the weekend."

Logan sighed. "So no Saturday night date. Okay."

It was amazing how great that made me feel, that he was already looking forward to a second date prior to even going on the first. "I must hug you now."

He held his arms out. "Hug away."

Stepping into them, I did my best to squeeze the stuffing out of him, my cheek pressed to his shoulder. "Thanks for being patient."

A chuckle rumbled in his chest. "I wouldn't call it patience as much as realizing you have a life to live."

"So do you." I lifted my head and leaned back. He didn't let go, meeting my eyes as his lips curved into a little smile.

"Mine's not as hectic as it used to be, and damn sure not as hectic as yours."

Which reminded me of something we'd talked about a few weeks before. "Did you talk to Terra about working at the office?"

Logan nodded. "I did, and she's okay with it."

"When are you going to talk to Mr. Whitehaven?"

"Probably next week. I have to decide who'll take over the garage if he hires me."

"Oh, yeah, that's an important decision." Was I hanging out in his arms too long? He didn't seem to mind. I damn sure didn't mind, because Logan's arms were a great place to be.

Even better when he bent his head slightly, inviting me to take advantage of his lips being close. I did take advantage, but only for a few seconds before drawing back again. More kissing, and I wouldn't want to send him out the door. "I'll see you tomorrow night."

"Okay." He pressed his cheek against mine, a soft rasp of a purr escaping, and released me. "Sleep well."

"You too."

I spent a few minutes doing a victory dance after closing the door behind him, happy I hadn't ruined things by asking for that rain check. Bone and Diablo joined in, prancing and grinning, infected by my happiness.

After my victory dance, I went to my home office. Funny thing: The more questions I received answers to, the more aware I became of others. Many of them were vague annoyances, not necessarily important. Yet, I had a sudden burning desire to find the answers to as many of them as possible.

Sitting at my desk, I picked up a pen and dragged the waiting legal pad in front of me. "Start simple."

What questions had bugged me for a while? "Ooh, I know."

I wrote "What is Mr. Whitehaven? Why is he so important in the supe community that they call him 'Lord'?"

I tapped the pen a few times before coming up with my next question: "Where/who is the dragon?"

That seemed like a good start, and I congratulated myself while re-reading the questions. "Hey, wait a minute."

White dragon. Whitehaven. No, just because Dr. Allen turned out to be Alleryn... But I'd seen my boss's eyes glow red a few times and he had pure white hair. Dragons breathed fire, right? And fire was partially red.

Couldn't dragons do magic too? I'd read fairytales as a kid, and thought I remembered one or two where the dragon masqueraded as a human. "Holy crap."

No, wait. That really wasn't enough evidence to decide my boss was Santo Trueno's resident dragon. Was it?

Then again, when I was a dog, I'd smelled Whitehaven's scent. It had been smoky and kind of metallic. And he did have all those treasures... "You know what? I'll just ask him privately when I have the chance."

It'd be cool to learn I was working for a dragon. Maybe not so cool if Mr. Whitehaven was the dragon, and blew a draconic gasket when I asked.

Shaking that out of my head, I moved on and wrote "Talk to Moira about the ancestors."

The why of my seeing them didn't really bother me. The dream was the issue: the White Queen jumping inside of and transforming me. That bothered me a lot, because of the empty spot in the circle of spectral tigers on Solstice Night.

However she'd done it, the missing tiger had helped save Logan. I didn't feel different, but what if she were trapped inside me or something? If she were, then getting her out seemed like the right thing to do. After all, the curse could be affecting her in some fashion.

"Okay, what else?" I didn't have to think about it, because only the biggie was left: "Who the hell cursed me this time, and why?"

I doubted there'd be an answer for that one before the end of the year, with only four days left. Overtaken by a yawn, I dropped the pen and decided it was bed time.

After making my rounds to check the front and back doors—it was too cold to have to worry about having opened windows—I called the dogs and picked up the two Chihuahuas for the trip upstairs. Leglin's room had become the whole pack's room, but the hound didn't mind. He slept with me anyway, since I didn't have a boyfriend staying overnight anymore.

Also, duty. Leglin was emphatic that his duty was to protect me. Funny, when it was a dog doing the protecting, I didn't argue much. Not even after Red's death.

Not that arguing with Leglin would work anyway. He'd sleep across my threshold if I didn't let him share the bed. He was that loyal.

I tucked Speck and Squishy into their bed, covering them with a soft throw. Bone and Diablo plopped onto their over-sized, therapeutic doggy beds. The people bed Leglin had asked for was still on my To Do list. "Night, guys. Sleep tight."

Contented sighs followed me out the door, putting a smile on my face. My hound waited by my bedroom door, and I patted his shoulder as I went through the doorway. "Come on."

It was a huge relief to change for bed without Merriven leering at me. Sliding between the sheets after face washing and teeth brushing, I made certain my alarm was on before rolling over to snuggle Leglin. "You didn't say anything about having a gargoyle coming to live with us."

"*It will be nice to have a partner.*"

I hid my smile by kissing the back of his head. "As long as you're cool with it, I guess I am."

His tail thump made the bed shiver. With a final squeeze, I rolled over onto my back and closed my eyes. Jogging time would come too early for my liking.

EIGHT

I woke up feeling like a million bucks, thanks to the lack of nightmares plaguing my sleep. Or maybe because the day would end in my first official date with Logan.

Thinking about that certainly put some pep into my morning jog. I even enjoyed the cold, crisp air while the dogs and I made our way around the property line. Seriously, aside from the "cursed by unknown assailant" thing, my life didn't look awful at the moment.

I had a good job, a fantastic place to call home, and my canine family to share it with. My closest neighbors weren't only friends, but extended family.

And unless we came up with a lead, or the boss assigned us another case, I had a free day ahead of me.

The sprint from drive entrance to house didn't feel like utter torture.

I was pouring a cup of coffee when my phone chimed to let me know a text message had arrived. It was from Logan: **Looking forward to tonight**.

Me too, I texted back, unable to control the smile spreading across my face. He responded with an emoticon, a red flower. We traded smiley faces then he texted **I'd better get to work**.

After I ate breakfast, I remembered I needed to make a couple of calls. First, Terra. She answered the phone before the first ring ended. "Hi."

"Hey, how does a sleepover tomorrow night and shopping Sunday sound?"

"It sounds great. Logan told me you'd be calling. Alanna's invited too, right?"

I'd promised Logan to include Alanna anytime I took Terra out, and I liked Alanna anyway. She was Dane's sister. "Yep, she's invited too. I'll have to pick up Tonya, so how about you two come over about five tomorrow? I'll call if something comes up and we need to make it later, okay?"

"Okay." An excited little chirp came through the phone. "This is going to be fun."

"Yes, it will. Talk to you later." Call over, that was one thing off my immediate To Do list. I called Tonya next, and she agreed. We spent ten minutes planning the sleepover. I hadn't had one in years, and even then, we'd mostly giggled over boys, watched scary movies, and given each other makeovers.

After talking to Tonya, it didn't seem much had changed. My Saturday night taken care of, I cleaned away my breakfast mess and wondered what to do with the rest of my day.

Dane called. "Anything new?"

"Not a thing on the case. You?"

"No. We could go look around where your thread ended. Maybe we'll find something."

There went my free day, but it didn't bother me. "Sure. Come on over and we'll go poke around."

"Okay, it ended here." I held up my forefinger to point to where the thread had run out. "Which is weird, because normally they're at ground level."

"That's eye-level for you." Dane circled to my left. "Does the change in height mean something?"

"I have no idea."

"Hm." He waved his hand above and below my finger. "I don't feel anything."

"Me neither." I kind of hated cases like this one, which looked as though it'd take weeks to solve. My longest-running case had taken almost four months, and had also involved a stolen item.

The problem was, the return of magic and supes had made crime-solving much more difficult. It was hard to determine motive when you didn't know if the culprit was human. Throw in the use of magic or beyond-human abilities, and it could be downright impossible to figure out whodunit.

Unless you had an edge, like us. But our "edges" didn't guarantee anything, as our current situation illustrated.

"Frustrating." Dane glared at the tip of my finger. "I don't know what we do next."

Dropping my hand to my side, I grinned. "Yes, you do. Let's go back to the car."

"Argh, time for 'what do we know'."

"Yep."

Once in my car, he began. "We know a magic mirror was stolen from the museum. We know who owns the mirror. We know the mirror was transported by shadows."

He fell silent while I started my car and pulled out of the parking lot. Once I'd merged with traffic, I prompted him. "And?"

"We know only a being with powerful magic can manipulate shadows. Which means our suspects are elves, demons, or gods."

I nodded. "Give me a motive for each type."

Dane thought about it for a few minutes. "Elves, well, it's a magic mirror. They collect magical artifacts. Could be power greed or collector's jealousy. Maybe even a personal vendetta against Celadine, because of elvish politics or something."

"Okay. Next?"

"Gods. No clue. Gods can do almost anything, so I can't think of a reason one would need to steal a magical artifact. Except to take it out of play or put it into play."

I glanced at him, and could feel my brow wrinkling. "What?"

"If Celadine was using the mirror, or maybe because she allowed humans access to it, a god may have decided to put a stop to it." Dane grinned. "Or, it wasn't being used and a god decided it should be, so took it and gave the mirror to someone who would use it."

"Huh, okay. Why would a god decide to do that?"

"Mischief? A reward to a devotee? I don't know. Gods are weird."

"Yeah." As though I didn't know that, having been used as a vessel by two. Their exit method had left a lot to be desired. "Okay, that leaves demons."

He shrugged. "Again, magic mirror. Demons could have a use for it."

A use we probably wouldn't like, but no need to say that. "You're lead. What's the next step?"

"Try to determine which suspect type is most likely? But I don't know how."

Cruising down the highway toward home, I tried to recall what I knew about the mirror. "In the story, the mirror only spoke truth, but it could tell the Evil Queen where Snow White was."

Dane snorted. "But that's a story, not real life. And the lady at the museum said the mirror talked a lot."

"Thorandryll told me the spirit in the mirror was put there by a god," I said, remembering.

"Well, maybe the same god took it back to release the spirit. Prison sentence over."

My turn to snort. "Possible, but is that plausible?"

"No clue."

"At least we have some angles to think about now. Good job, partner." I tossed him a smile, which Dane returned.

We needed more clues to advance on the case, and none appeared forthcoming. Once home, Dane decided to stick around for a while, so we played with the dogs to enjoy the weak afternoon sun.

Leglin joined Bone and Dane in a rousing game of fetch. Diablo watched, but didn't play. I needed to catch my breath from the laughter and romping, so I joined him and the Chihuahuas on the porch.

Squishy and Speck squabbled over the tug-o-war rope toy I was sliding across the floor for them.

"*Mine.*"

"*Mine.*" Speck growled, slapping at her with his tiny paw. Ears perked to the point that the tips met, she bounced at him, forcing him away from the toy.

Then they were racing back and forth, barking and chasing each other, the toy forgotten. I moved to the steps to get out of their way.

Sitting next to Diablo, I put my arm around him and scratched his chest. He grunted and leaned against me.

"Why aren't you playing?"

"*Playing's for pups.*"

"Bone and Leglin aren't pups."

Diablo grunted again.

"Playing's good for everyone," I said.

The black pit bowed his head and mumbled, "*I don't know how.*"

"You played in the snow at the park." I moved to scratching behind his ear.

"*We were knocking each other down. I know how to do that.*"

Of course he did. He'd been trained to fight, so knocking an opponent off his feet had been part of the training. I hugged him. "I didn't know how to play when I was a dog. But there's an extra tennis ball."

"*Can't catch it.*"

Diablo had a habit of making my heart hurt. I thought he'd settled in well considering his past. He'd been super careful with the little ones. In fact, all the ex-fighters had.

"We can go around back and practice," I suggested, not really expecting him to take me up on the offer.

He watched Bone leap into the air, catching the ball Dane had thrown, and twitched. Licking his chops, he said, "*Okay.*"

I hugged him. "Let me put the little ones inside and get the ball."

Five minutes later, we were in the back yard. I held up the tennis ball. "We'll start easy. I'll just toss it in the air, and you try to catch it."

"*Sure.*" Diablo was tense, his tail tucked.

"No pressure, okay? I bet it's hard to learn to catch like this. I can't even catch popcorn with my mouth." I saw his tail relax a bit. "It'll take practice."

"*Right.*"

He missed the first three tosses, but didn't give up in disgust, to my pleasure. Instead, he relaxed and kept trying. The seventh, he caught, his ears flattening and then perking in surprise.

"Yay!" I scratched his neck. "You did it. Give me the ball."

"*No.*" Diablo backed away, his tail high and beginning to wag.

"Come on, I can't throw it for you if I don't have it."

"*You can have it if you catch me.*" He took off running; laughing, I gave chase.

NINE

By six-forty, I was ready for my date, and wondering why the hell I felt so nervous. It wasn't as though I were going out with a stranger or someone I barely knew. Logan had seen me in all sorts of situations. We'd already had a sort-of date, had even cuddled and slept together. We didn't need to do anything impress each other. He'd seen me with morning hair.

Yet, I had to leave the living room window, where I'd been standing to watch for his arrival, to go wash my hands. My palms were sweating like crazy. I went to the kitchen, washed and dried my hands, and seriously considered a trip upstairs to rub some antiperspirant on my palms. Sweaty hands were gross.

The dogs were lying around the living room, and Bone stuck his head over the back of the couch. "*Logan's here.*"

"Crap."

My white pit cocked his head. "*I thought we liked him?*"

"We do. Sorry, it's weird people stuff." I hurried to the front door, hearing the rumble of Logan's dark green, classic muscle car as I got there, and opened the door. He was just pulling into the parking area in front of the garage. "Crap. Over-eager, much?"

Since I already had the door opened, I waved at him before grabbing my coat and purse. "See you later, guys. Keep an eye on the littles. Leglin, you're in charge. Bye."

By the time I stepped out and shut the door, Logan was out of his car. "Hi."

"Hi." I began to put my coat on while heading for the stairs, and had to stop when it tangled around my legs. "Just a minute."

"I thought I was supposed to come to the door?" He walked toward me. I dropped my purse, trying to wrestle my coat on. "You want some help with that?"

Totally flustered, I stopped struggling. "Yes, please."

He climbed the steps, picked up my purse, and took my coat. "There's this trick to it. You put one arm in at a time."

I accepted my purse when he held it out to me, my face warm, and turned while he shook out the coat. "Really? One arm at a time?"

"Yeah, and it helps if the arm's not the one with the hand holding something at the end."

Slipping my empty hand into a sleeve, I had to laugh. "Sorry. I'm nervous. That's stupid, isn't it?"

"No." He waited while I switched my purse to my other hand. "I'm a little nervous too."

"But we shouldn't be." I found the other sleeve, and he let go once the coat was settled. Turning around, I asked, "Should we?"

"Probably not, but," Logan smiled, lifting his hands and spreading them. "This is our First Official Date."

"Right, but we've slept together." I felt like disappearing as the words left my mouth. "I mean, well, yeah, we did sleep together. There was cuddling. It's dumb to be nervous after that."

He chuckled. "Tell that to the butterflies in my stomach."

"At least I'm not the only one who has them." I hoped I didn't end up saying any more stupid things. Anxiety had a way of running my mouth without checking with my brain first.

"Shall we?" Logan cocked his arm for me to take hold.

I smiled. "Let's."

Some women didn't like men doing things like opening doors for them, but I didn't have a problem with him walking me around, and opening the passenger door. I liked it when men behaved like gentlemen, and did those little things. Logan even bent and tucked my coat inside the car before shutting the door.

Once behind the steering wheel, he glanced at me. "I forgot to tell you that you look great."

"I won't hold it against you." But I was pleased he'd noticed I'd gone to more effort than usual with my hair and makeup. "You look great too."

"What, this old thing?" He plucked at the front of his teal shirt. "Had it for ages, but thanks."

"Isn't that supposed to be my line?"

"You missed your cue." Logan started the engine. "I hope you're hungry."

I hoped my idiotic nervousness didn't result in me throwing up whatever we had for dinner. "Starving. Where are we going?"

"It's a surprise." He was backing out at a curve, to turn the car around.

He was wearing black jeans and the long-sleeved teal button-up. Nice, but not super fancy. I had on black palazzo pants and a burgundy, trapeze-cut, nearly sheer top over a black cami. And, of course, the Tear Petra had given me, tucked inside my top, and my faux tiger coat. "Am I overdressed?"

"You look great."

I laughed. "That wasn't my question."

"You're not overdressed," he said, finishing his three-point turn. "How was work today?"

"Frustrating." I filled him in on our lack of tangible progress, and by the time I'd finished yapping, we were pulling into the parking lot of Le Rêve Sauvage. "Ooh. You're spoiling me."

"You enjoyed that lunch so much, I thought this was a good dinner choice."

"You thought right." My nervousness had disappeared during the drive.

The restaurant was decorated in an Art Deco style, all black and white with glints of silver, and had a quiet, relaxing atmosphere. The maître d' seated us at a small, round table for two to one side of the dining area. We ordered Suprême de Faisan Sauce Savagnin et Morilles after discussing the pros and cons of just about every offering on the menu. Logan deferred to me on the wine, and I chose a Pinot Noir.

Once the wine was poured, I couldn't pick a conversation topic. Work was out, having already talked about it. And who wants to spend their date talking about work constantly anyway? "How's everyone settling in?"

"The euphoria would probably knock you out. We haven't had a single complaint yet, about anything." Logan's smile was brighter than the flame of the candle in the center of our table. "I think this is the first time since the clan was formed that everyone is happy."

"That's fantastic. You did a great job." I knew he'd had to work with elves to plan the pocket realm, and had seen the results on Solstice Night for myself. "Exactly how much room is in there?"

"I don't know, because pocket realms are kind of fluid about that. Plenty," he said. "You could run for days before you were looped back."

I raised my eyebrows. "Looped back?"

"Yes." Logan leaned forward. "The outer boundary is kind of an illusion. It'll look like the land keeps going, but when you hit the boundary, the magic will sort of transition you back to the entrance."

"Even if you don't go straight?"

He nodded. "Even then."

"My brain doesn't want to wrap around that." I'd learned that supes had labeled psychics "natural mages" before the Melding, but still didn't feel like what I did was actual magic. There was no way I could create an entire place out of nothing, or do something like transform other people into dogs.

Logan chuckled. "It hurts mine too. I'm just happy it works."

"What about adding new houses?"

"That's built into the magic." He sat back, took a sip of wine, and tried to explain. "A pocket realm is tuned to its inhabitants. If we need more houses, they'll appear. Everything will move without really moving."

"Okay, my head's going to start hurting." I wondered why Nick's father had decreed a house would be built. Did their territory differ from other pocket realms? If so, why? Then again, did I really want to know if they did? Probably not. Explanations of magic usually resulted in migraines, because I couldn't grasp the hows and whys of how magic worked.

Logan didn't mind my call for a subject change. "What would you like to do after dinner?"

"What are the options?"

"Dancing, a movie, or there's a carnival in the Barrows. We could go for a walk at a park, or at home..." He smiled. "Entirely up to you."

"There's a carnival in the Barrows? What's a vampire carnival like?"

"Weirder side shows, but there's rides."

"That might be fun. Would you mind if we stopped by to see Tase for a few minutes?" It hadn't been a week yet, but I thought it might be rude to go down there and not stop by.

"No, don't mind at all."

Our dinner was served then, dropping conversation down to the food, which was delicious.

The vampire carnival was wilder than I expected, and Logan was right about the sideshows being weirder. Human carnivals didn't offer things like sex shows or vampire feedings. I couldn't believe people paid to let vampires bite them, no matter how sexy the vamp was. Or, for that matter, to watch them having sex with each other. It was definitely not a family-friendly carnival.

We avoided those tents, sticking to the rides and midway games. Logan won a dark purple and lavender stuffed bear for me at the dart game. The bear wasn't small, but large enough to make carrying it awkward. "I'll put him in the corner of my bedroom, and his name shall be Mr. Pansy."

"Pansy?" Logan hefted the bear onto his back, holding onto its arms over his shoulders.

"It's logical, I promise. Pansies come in the same shades of purple." I stroked my new stuffie's side. "He's so soft. Thank you."

"You're welcome." We left the dart game's front and walked down the midway. "What next?"

"Ferris wheel?" I hooked my finger through his belt loop, since his hands weren't free.

"Sounds like a plan."

The loading platform for the Ferris wheel wasn't crowded. Apparently, humans preferred the kinkier sideshows. Go figure.

"Do you want to sit with me, or Mr. Pansy?" Logan asked once he'd put the bear on one of the benches inside our cab.

"With you, of course."

"Just checking. He has me beat in the cuddly department."

"But he can't cuddle back. He's a cuddlee, not a cuddler." We sat on the other bench, and I pulled Logan's arm over my shoulders, scooting closer to him. "You can cuddle back. You win."

He kissed my temple before saying, "Sorry, Mr. Pansy."

The ride began, our cab rocking as it rose. I sighed. "These are supposed to be romantic. Jerky movements aren't romantic."

Logan surveyed the cab. "We're in a metal cage."

"It's called a cab."

"It's still a metal cage."

I laughed. "Okay, yeah, but it's a cage for safety reasons, so that no one falls out."

Of course, since there was an opening in the top half of the door to the cab, someone could jump out. And I'd seen someone do that, in the past. The memory killed my smile.

"What's wrong?"

"I was remembering Rose Middleton."

"The woman at the fair."

"Yeah."

"You can't save everyone, but the important thing is, you try. And you did save a lot of people that time."

"We saved a lot of people."

Logan gently squeezed my shoulders. "Okay, we."

I was the worst date ever, killing the fun we'd been having, but was now stuck in a conversational corner. An apology seemed my best bet. "Sorry."

"For what, remembering a victim?"

"Well, yeah. We're supposed to be having fun."

He pulled his arm from around me, and turned a little to face me, reaching for my hand. I turned too, so our knees touched. Logan looked at me for a few seconds. "Here's the thing: I do have fun with you, but I don't expect everything to be fun all the time. Life doesn't cooperate like that. I'm more than okay with sharing the rough stuff too, whenever it comes up. It may not be fun, but it is a sign of trust. I'll take trust over fun any day."

"Okay, seriously now, you really are taking classes in how to say the right thing all the time, aren't you?"

"No classes, promise." Logan shrugged. "Maybe I'm just saying the things you already know, but need to hear from someone else."

"I didn't already know having an attack of the blues on a date wouldn't bother you." At least, I didn't think I knew that, but then again, I'd unloaded my baggage on Logan before, and he'd never flinched.

"You know we're friends," he said. "And good friends don't mind sharing the good and the bad stuff."

"Point."

"All I'm saying is, don't worry about sharing whatever you want to with me."

"Thanks. The same goes for you." It was entirely possible I was the luckiest woman in the world. Or perhaps, the most manipulated by gods one.

Not liking that thought, I decided it was time to return to having fun. "Can we get back to where we were snuggling on this romantic ride?"

"We can." Logan shifted, putting his arm around me again, a huge smile lighting up his face.

We left the carnival about eleven, and decided to walk to visit Tase.

The Barrows were more active and crowded at night. Vampires required their six hours of recharging during daylight hours, though some did need to hit the coffin just before sunrise. Others wouldn't rise until after the sun set.

Even then, I'd learned their deady-bye times varied from season to season, based on the amount of daylight. That had been a downer for me, since I'd thought those times were set in stone.

But no, only that each slept at a full six hours was a firm rule. Because of that, there were always vampires awake in the Barrows, even during the day. They just had to stay out of the sun.

The tourists were out in full force at night, too, dressed for partying. We passed groups of young adults and older teens, and held hands to keep from being separated. "I don't get it."

"Don't get what?" Logan glanced at me, Mr. Pansy tucked under his other arm.

"Why so many people want to mingle with vampires. What's the allure?"

"They're different."

"Yeah, but this different is also dangerous, and those two things usually cause fear. Fear can turn to hatred, and that tends to result in prejudice." Or so said my twenty-one years of conscious experience. "And humans have a habit of wanting to be the same, or trying to force people to be like them."

He thought about that for a few steps. "As far as I know, that's not something that only applies to humans. Every species forms groups. Like-minded groups, that feel they're right or special in some fashion."

"I guess. Maybe I'm missing the vamp groupie gene." Probably the elf groupie gene too. "Because I did not like getting bitten and having my blood sucked."

"Some people do." Logan guided me through a knot of drunken revelers. "Couldn't tell you why."

"I also don't get the allure of immortality. Who wants to live forever? At some point, it has to become boring."

"Not if you don't remember all of it."

I made a face. "How can they forget?"

"Brains aren't limitless storage boxes, not even for elves or vampires. Hell, I can't remember what I ate last week, or every single thing I did each day. Can you?"

"No."

Logan smiled. "Pretty sure they can't, either. But we do remember the big events, and the special ones."

"True, but after a few thousand years, those kinds of events are going to repeat, aren't they?"

"I suppose, but they won't be exactly the same."

Wrinkling my nose, I said, "I still think it'd get boring."

"So do I, but then, I'm not an elf or vampire."

By then we'd reached the correct street to turn down. One or more of the gargoyles' neighbors appeared to be having parties, judging by the lights, noise, and groups of people dotting the street.

The gates were closed when we reached the late Esme's estate. I looked up at the gargoyle perched on the left wall. "Hello. We've come to visit Tase."

The gargoyle came to life to look down. "You may enter. Please close the gate behind you."

"Sure. Thanks." The double gates had a simple lift and drop latch. Logan reset the latch once we'd walked through.

A small blur flew toward us. I hastily lifted my hand. "Hey, Tase."

"Hello." The baby gargoyle landed neatly on my palm. "Who is he?"

"This is my friend, Logan."

"Hello, Logan."

"Hi, Tase."

The little guy settled his wings and sat up. "I'm pleased to meet you."

"Same here."

I wondered if Logan was as charmed by Tase as I was. "Mama says we can sit in the garden to visit."

"Okay." I patted my purse. "I brought a sponge."

We'd stopped on the way to the Barrows to buy one.

"Neat." Tase leaped from my hand, his wings flapping. He flew a circle around Mr. Pansy's head. "Sponges are really big."

I giggled. "That's not the sponge. It's a stuffed animal."

"Then what is that?"

"It's a toy bear."

"Oh. This way." Tase banked, turned, and flew down the walk. We followed. He led us to a small, grassy square with a round stone table and cushion-topped benches.

Tase landed on the table and watched as Logan sat Mr. Pansy on one of the benches. I pulled out a small bottle of water and the cellophane-wrapped sponge before sitting down. Logan sat beside me, the faint curve of his lips hinting at amusement.

"This is a sponge." I opened both of my show-and-tell props and demonstrated the sponge's ability to soak up spilled water. After that, we tried to explain why we were carrying a stuffed animal around, and chit-chatted for a little while. Finally, I said, "it's getting late. We should go."

"May I have the sponge?"

"Sure."

Tase's tail whipped left and right as he wrinkled his tiny snout into a grin. "Thank you."

"You're welcome. Do you want me to carry it for you?"

"I can carry it. When will you come see me again?"

"In a few days." I stroked his back with my finger, making a note to bring him another present. Something better than a kitchen sponge. "See you then, and please tell your mother we said hello."

"I will. Bye." The baby gargoyle pounced on the sponge, digging his claws into it, and unfurled his wings. "Bye, Logan."

"Good night, Tase." Logan slid off the bench to retrieve Mr. Pansy. I rose, collecting the wrapper and empty water bottle.

Tase managed to lift the sponge two inches off the table, and slowly, drunkenly, flapped away.

"How cute is he?" I asked when we began walking.

"Extremely."

"Do you think he'd like some blocks or toy cars?"

"Maybe." Logan reached for my hand. "You might have to explain them to him."

When we reached the gate, I paused. "How safe is it here, with all the gargoyles? At night, I mean."

"It's probably the safest place in the city. Why?"

"Safe enough to bring my brothers to meet Tase?"

He nodded. "Yes. Gargoyles are particularly fond of children, from the stories I've heard."

"Cool." All I'd have to do is talk Dad and Betty into allowing me to bring the boys. Probably easier thought of than done. Shelving the idea for future consideration, I unlatched the gate.

<hr />

"I had a really good time." We were at my front door. Logan had refused my offer of coffee, mentioning he knew my weekend would be busy.

"So did I. I guess we'll see each other at the ball."

"Yeah." Where I'd be someone else's date. Stupid elf.

"Okay." Logan touched my cheek, tilting his head, and I accepted his implicit invitation, meeting his lips.

There were few things I enjoyed more than kissing him, though I suspected the physical stuff would only get better as our relationship progressed.

"Good night," he said, once the kiss ended.

"Night." Watching him leave, I couldn't stop smiling. If nothing else in my life was going right, at least this one thing—Logan and me—seemed to be.

TEN

I didn't sleep in the next morning, knowing I probably would Sunday thanks to my overnight guests.

After jogging, shower, and breakfast, I spent a couple of hours washing clothes before going grocery shopping. By the time I'd unloaded and put things away, it was time to go pick up Tonya.

I drove, in case she wanted to stop somewhere before we headed home, and she did. Once we'd said "Bye" to Mom, and the teen's husky, Kyra, and were in my car, Tonya said, "Video store?"

"Logan hooked up my TV to the home network. We can rent online."

"Okay. Dollar store?"

"For what?"

The teen bounced. "Nail stuff and makeup. How else are we going to do makeovers?"

"Okay." On the street, I asked, "How's the studies going?"

She turned a huge, bright smile my way. "They think I'm nearly ready for a familiar."

"That's a big step, right?"

"Huge step. I'll be able to do more than light candles and mix the easy potions with a familiar."

"Awesome." I wondered how long she'd been comatose after the Melding. Tonya would've been eight or nine when it happened. From past conversations, I knew most of my witch buddies had slept for a month or two. All of them, except Tonya, were a few years older than me. Deciding it wasn't too intrusive, I asked, "How long did the Melding knock you out for?"

"Forty-three days." Her smile was gone. "I missed my mom's funeral."

"I'm sorry." Crap, I shouldn't have asked.

"Wasn't your fault. We'd left the fireworks show early, trying to avoid traffic. A drunk driver ran a red light." Tonya lifted her shoulder. "She hit us. I remember the car spinning around, and hitting my head on the door. Then I woke up in the hospital all that time later."

Ah. That's why no one had realized she was a witch before. "They thought your coma was because of the accident."

"Yeah. I did too." She let her shoulder fall and grinned. "But no, I'm one of the freaks."

I lifted my hand from the shifter knob, and made a fist. "Freak power."

"Freak power." Tonya fist-bumped me, and we both laughed.

Terra and Alanna were waiting on the front porch when we arrived. Both bounced up to hurry to the car, and hugs ensued all around.

It seemed sort of funny they were excited about the sleepover. The clan held regular gatherings, and they spent a lot of time together every day.

Then again, maybe that was why, because spending a night elsewhere was unusual. Even if the elsewhere wasn't all that far from home.

"I bought stuff to make pizzas," I said once we were inside.

"I'll help." Terra left Alanna at the dinette table with Tonya, ignoring the lure of makeup and twenty different colors of nail polish.

"I cheated. Picked up readymade crusts."

"Okay." We pulled out all the makings while Tonya talked Alanna into being the first makeover victim.

Terra started slicing the bell peppers. "How was the big date?"

"We had a great time." My instant smile caused an eruption of giggles from them.

"Details," Tonya demanded.

I shook my head. "There aren't any to share. We had dinner, went to the carnival in the Barrows, and visited the gargoyles before he brought me home."

Alanna, her eyes closed to allow Tonya to apply dark purple eyeshadow, said, "Logan was in a really good mood for that to have been all."

"Well, we did cuddle on the Ferris wheel, and there may have been some kissing."

"Just kissing? No groping? How many bases?" Tonya paused to take a look at her handiwork.

"Nosy. I don't remember which base is what, but that's all that happened. We cuddled, kissed, and held hands a lot."

"Ooh."

I stopped dicing onions. "Please tell me I'm not the only one dating anybody."

"You are." Terra sighed. "Devon's too afraid of Logan to hold my hand, much less kiss me, and it's not like we could go anywhere alone anyway."

"You have the whole territory," Alanna said. "Have a picnic."

"Yeah, and all the snoopy clan in it. I'm talking about going to the movies and stuff."

Tonya broke in. "If that guy's scared of Logan, maybe he's not the right guy."

"But I like him."

"Yeah, but," Tonya shook her head. "I wouldn't want to date a guy who wasn't willing to take a few risks. Seriously, what would Logan do to him just for holding your hand, or kissing you? It's not like he'd rearrange Devon's face for that." She looked from Alanna to Terra, and then me. "Would he?"

"No." My response made her nod.

"See? Devon wouldn't even be taking a real risk there."

Terra frowned. "I guess."

Sensing her unhappiness, I changed the subject. "We're doing personal pizzas. What do you girls want on yours?"

After a night of scary movies, too much makeup, some really strange hairstyles, and a lot of junk food, I woke up to discover Tonya and Terra had given me a toothpaste mask while I slept.

In retaliation, I woke them up by pouring cold water on them. They erupted into shrieking wakefulness and chaos followed as they chased me around the house, trying to smack me with their soggy pillows. The dogs joined in, barking and snatching at the pillows.

Finally, I had to call a halt. "We're running out of time."

Terra threw her pillow at me. I ducked it, but not Tonya's pillow, launched directly after, and was hit smack in the face. "Ow. Okay, okay."

We cleaned up, had breakfast, and prepared for our trip to the mall.

The mall was packed, but at least parking wasn't an issue for us. I'd teleported us to a spot around the side of the anchor store, where there weren't any doors. Not much foot traffic there. "Okay, ladies, let's stay together. No wandering away from the group."

"We know," Tonya and Terra chorused, before trading grins.

"Because Mom and Logan will both kill me if I lose either of you." I checked the inside pocket of my leather jacket, making certain my wallet was secure. My purse was at home. The first few days after Christmas were always full of people returning or exchanging Christmas presents they didn't want, which made the mall a choice spot for pickpockets to work.

No one in our little group was carrying a purse. I'd seen Alanna put her wallet in the inside pocket of her jacket before we'd left.

Tonya grabbed Terra's hand, pulling her forward. "Let's go."

I followed them with Alanna. "Teenagers. Shopping's their drug."

She chuckled, hooking her arm around mine. "Let's pretend we're teenagers too."

"I can do that." Probably easier than she could, thanks to my long, Melding-induced nap. "I just wish this shopping trip wasn't because of that damn elf."

"You're not flattered at all by his attention."

"Nope." I had been, once or twice, because Thorandryll was gorgeous. Yet, he was also a lying schemer, which had rubbed all the shiny off having his attention. Our recent meeting had only solidified my decision to never get romantically involved with the elf. "Maybe if he was actually sincere, but I know he's not. It's all political with him."

"Usually is with elves." Alanna caught the door as the two girls went inside ahead of us. "Okay, fun time."

"Right."

We meandered through the crowd, window shopping as we went. My phone dinged, and I pulled it from my pocket to read a text from Logan: **Having fun?**

Loads, I typed. **They pasted me.**

Then I had to explain what that meant, which made it clear the toothpaste mask had been Tonya's idea. I noticed the other three had moved to another storefront while I was busy. **Gotta go. We're running out of time to shop.**

Okay, bye. He added a flower emoticon.

Shoving my phone back into my pocket, I hurried after the other three, and bumped into a man. "Oh, sorry."

He shot me an annoyed look, and I flinched away, because his eyes were solid black. The human-suited demon hurried past without doing anything else.

Curious, I turned around to watch him, and wondered why he hadn't attacked me. Had they decided to let bygones be bygones?

That would be cool by me, except for the fact that a demon had just passed, wearing a human. Or what was left of a human.

After one incident, killing a demon and hearing a mental scream, I'd asked Mr. Whitehaven if possessed humans could be saved. He'd said no. That their souls were ripped out and couldn't return, because the bodies were too tainted.

Basically, demons murdered the owners of the bodies they possessed, which meant a killer was wandering around the mall. If there was one demon, there were probably be others.

"Cordi," Tonya called, and I walked over to join them in front of the boutique. "Look at that dress."

"It's nice." I glanced away, but could no longer see the demon. The urge to give chase struck, but I'd promised Logan I wouldn't let Terra out of my sight. He probably wouldn't like it if I took her demon hunting.

"I love that one." Terra pointed through the glass to a slinky, gold dress adorning a headless mannequin. "What do you think, Alanna?"

"You should try it on."

Into the shop we went. The girls examined the gold dress, while I tried to decide if we should leave.

A saleswoman appeared, and stripped the mannequin for Terra to try on the dress. Alanna touched my arm. "I'll go with her."

"Okay, thanks." I let Tonya pull me around the shop to look at other dresses, nodding and mumbling in response to her comments about each.

The auburn-haired teen witch finally planted her hands on her hips. "What the heck's wrong with you? Shopping, fancy dresses, and fun. Remember?"

"Yeah, totally." Crap, I wasn't being a good hostess.

"So what's ruining the fun vibe?"

I sighed, and decided to tell her. "I saw a demon a few minutes ago."

Tonya's eyes widened. "Where?"

"Out there." I waved my hand at the shop's front. "He bumped into me, and kept going."

Her hands dropped from her hips. "I have a banishing potion."

"You do?"

She nodded, patting the pocket of her coat. "David and Jo said we should have one on us at all times. Just in case."

"Nice. Keep it handy."

"We're not going after it?"

I laughed. "Are you kidding? I'd be murdered twice, once by Mom, and the other by Logan, if I took you and Terra demon hunting."

"But..."

"No buts. If I see it again, you can banish him." My promise mollified her.

"Okay." Tonya turned her head as Alanna and Terra exited a fitting room. "Do we tell them?"

"I guess we'd better." Not that I wanted to ruin their fun, yet I didn't want a surprise demon attack to be a true surprise either.

"What do you think?" Terra did a catwalk turn, her head held high. The gold dress was a strapless sheath that clung from chest to a few inches below her hips. The rest of it swished and stilled, touching the floor.

"You look awesome," I said. Tonya clapped her hands and whistled. "You should definitely get it."

"I agree." Alanna's smile hinted at pride. "We'll need to find the right shoes."

Smoothing her hands over the dress, Terra nodded. "Have you found one yet?"

"Uh, not yet. Something..."

"Cordi saw a demon," Tonya blurted out. The other two lost their smiles.

"It's not out there now." I shrugged. "And it ignored me, so I don't think we're in trouble, but it's up to you if we keep shopping or leave."

Terra nibbled on her bottom lip, looking at Alanna, who was busy looking at the passing crowd beyond the shop's glass front.

"You have to find a dress," Tonya said. "You're already cutting it close, since the ball's tonight."

Alanna was frowning. "Are you sure it was a demon?"

"Yeah, saw the black eyes."

"What?"

"Don't know why, but their eyes look solid black to me."

"Interesting." She touched the ends of her dark brown hair. "If we stay alert, I think we'll be okay."

"Sure. I can teleport us, or call my hound, if something does happen," I agreed.

"I'll keep watch while you look for a dress," Alanna said.

Tonya went with Terra to the changing room. I hoped she wouldn't have to use the potion in her pocket.

Roughly an hour later, we left the boutique with dress bags, and in my case, a few hundred dollars deeper in credit debt. I'd chosen a sleeveless, dark blue dress, the skirt long and flowy. It was plain compared to Terra's choice, but then I wasn't a capital Q queen.

Also, I didn't want to glam things up so much that Thorandryll thought I was trying to impress him or anything. Because then he'd think I was playing hard to get, instead of being honest about the "not happening" thing.

Our next stop was a shoe store, and I sighed when I realized that once again, nothing had a price tag on it. The stupid dinner date was costing more than I wanted to spend on an evening of being trapped as the elf's date.

ELEVEN

At six pm, my doorbell rang. I took a last look in the mirror, checking my makeup and wondering if I was underdressed for hobnobbing with Santo Trueno's elite.

Probably, but nothing left to do about it now. Hurrying downstairs, I shushed the Chihuahuas, who were running in circles around the sofa while barking. "*Door! Door!*"

Leglin, Bone, and Diablo were sitting in a line in front of the door. Amused, I dodged around them to answer it.

Thorandryll looked absolutely gorgeous in black tie. Momentarily tongue-tied, I smiled as he lifted a smallish, golden box. "I believe it's customary to bring flowers."

"Right." I checked, and yes, he had a boutonniere of a white rose and baby's breath pinned to his jacket.

"Come in."

"Thank you." He stepped inside, noting the dogs watching, and smiled. "Good evening, gentlemen."

It struck me then, the disconnect between how he treated animals and shifters. He was polite to animals, or had been every time I'd seen him interact with them.

He was either rude to, or ignored, shifters. Kethyrdryll had told me it was stung pride over a woman, back when Thorandryll was young. Dude had had more than enough years to get past that, but he hadn't. Why?

Thorandryll opened the box and presented the corsage it held with a flourish. "I hope it pleases you."

"It's lovely." It was, a little bouquet of miniature white roses on a background of baby's breath and greenery. I stood still and let him pin it on me, while trying to ignore the high school prom vibe the situation caused.

It wasn't as though I'd gone to a prom. My "lost years" hadn't stopped once I'd woken from my coma. Two more were spent returning to normal physically, and learning to handle my abilities.

Twenty-three years old, and I still felt fifteen on a regular basis. Like a kid trying to pretend to be an adult. Most of the time, I thought I pulled off the charade well. Possibly because when people looked at me, they saw a grown woman.

None of them saw the awkward teenager who felt cheated out of the experiences she should've had. Fast forward was fine for commercials, but it sucked rotten goose eggs for real life.

Thorandryll was staring at me. I blinked, realizing he'd finished, and was standing with his arms down at his sides.

"Is something troubling you?"

"Kind of. Not you though. Just...life, I guess."

He tilted his head. "Life in general, or something in particular?"

I touched the corsage, the tiny roses velvet against my fingertips. "Mom doesn't have any photos of me dressed up for school dances. No prom photos, because when I should've been at my junior prom, I was in a coma. Senior prom, I was a walking skeleton who kept setting things on fire or freezing them."

"You're angry that you weren't allowed the experiences you expected to have."

I looked him in the eye. "Wouldn't you be?"

He nodded. "Of course."

"Not just angry, but sad." I sighed. "Doesn't matter. It's not like I'll get a do-over. No one's going to give me back those years."

"I am truly sorry for your loss," he said, abruptly turning toward the coat rack and taking down my faux tiger coat. "I presume you wish to wear this one?"

"Yes, thanks."

Keeping my eyes lowered, I put on my coat with his help. "Guard the house, guys. Don't close the little ones in a room." Tail thumps and lolling tongues answered me. "See you when I get home."

Thorandryll offered his arm once we were on the porch and I'd locked the door. I accepted the gesture, feeling uncomfortable with my oversharing.

A white limo waited in the driveway, its hood pointed to the road. I wondered how the chauffer had maneuvered it around, without driving onto the winter-crisped grass. Probably magic, since the chauffer was another elf.

How different would I be, if I'd grown up knowing I'd develop my abilities, instead of having them dumped on me? Maybe I'd have been as arrogant as any elf.

Nah, no way, not with my mom. She had no problem bursting arrogance bubbles when necessary.

"Champagne?"

"Huh? Oh, no thank you." I needed to quit wool-gathering, or risk setting the habit of being a terrible date. Not that I intended to be a fun date for the elf. Publicly friendly, sure. I had promised to play nice.

He poured a glass, took a sip, and began to talk. "This will be an interesting evening. The attendees are the elite of Santo Trueno, from both human and supernatural communities."

"A bunch of people impressed with themselves" is how I interpreted that. "I didn't think you counted shifters as important."

"We all have to live together, regardless of our preferences."

"Prejudices, you mean."

Thorandryll frowned. "I thought we'd agreed to be on friendly terms this evening."

"Yes, but that doesn't mean I'm suddenly blind and deaf to some things. Besides, we're not in public yet." In fact, we were just turning out of the drive. "Seriously, what is your problem with shifters?"

"They're animals. Animals that believe themselves equals of true people."

"Funny. You like animals, and treat them like people. I've seen you do that. But people who can turn themselves into animals..."

He interrupted. "You don't understand. The first to shift their shapes weren't humans. They were animals. Animals who loved their human masters, and wished to emulate them."

I had no idea what expression was on my face, because I didn't know what to think about his statement. "Oh. But that was a really long time ago."

"Time doesn't change what they are."

"Shifters."

"Perversions of the natural order."

I sniffed. "Maybe to you, but not to me."

"You strongly remind me of those you're descended from. They thought the shifters' evolution a miracle."

"Isn't it? Sounds like one to me."

"Animals aren't people," he insisted. "They are companions, pets, useful tools, and food, but they are not people."

"Shifters aren't just," I did air quotes for "just", "animals, and haven't been since the first one changed. We're in a new millennium here, one of a few that have passed since then. You need to get with the times."

Thorandryll glared for a few seconds before reluctantly smiling. "My brother has said the same, though less bluntly."

"I like Kethyrdryll. He has common sense." I shrugged. "Anyway, it was nice that you decided to include the shifter leaders."

"You believe I lack common sense?"

"I think you're so used to being important, you have a hard time relating to anyone else, except those you believe are important too."

Instead of glaring, he looked thoughtful. "Kethyrdryll has expressed a similar opinion."

As though I needed more reasons to like his brother. I changed the subject. "Who else is going to be there?"

"The Mayor, city council members, wealthy citizens, and of course, leaders of all the various groups. Many of the vampire council will be present."

I hoped Derrick was one of them. "Why'd you invite the coven?"

"Your friends may be young, but they're becoming known among those who matter. They'll eventually take a place among the elite."

"They may not want to."

He chuckled. "People with power seldom have a choice."

"I have power, and I'm not one of the elite."

"Of course you are, and this will be your debut among your equals."

I stared at him. "Yeah, right."

"You doubt me. I suggest you pay attention tonight, to how others react to you."

Crap, what had I gotten myself into? "Wait a minute. You freaking planned this. Showing up to a big deal dinner party with me as your date...son of a...that's going to send some messages, isn't it?"

"Of course."

"Ooh, you'd better be glad I promised to play nice."

"I'm grateful you have the habit of keeping promises. Though it would've been more favorable if we were lovers."

"I'm two seconds away from throwing my shoe at your face." God, he was unbelievable.

He laughed. "I'm merely pointing out that certain people would feel more comfortable knowing that you're less of a, what's the phrase? Ah, a wild card."

"Because if we were a couple they'd think you were in charge? Right." I drawled out the last word. "Like that would ever happen, you being the boss of me."

"Sometimes it's a useful illusion for others to have," he said. "Since you feel so strongly about the matter, I'm settling for the illusion of friendship between us."

I still wanted to smack him between his pretty blue eyes with the heel of my shoe. "If we're ever going to be friends, you have to stop playing games. I'm not a chess piece."

"You're not friends with the Rex, but you are allied with his Pride."

"I'm friends with his son, Connor."

Thorandryll lifted his glass. "You're friends with my brother and my healer."

"Well, yeah." The limo was slowing, and I glanced out the window. We were in a line, heading toward his sidhe. "But unless you stop playing games, I'm not going to be your friend."

"We don't have to be friends to be allies."

"It helps, a lot."

"But it's not absolutely necessary."

I sighed. "How's your mom?"

He blinked. "Queen Maeve is well. Why?"

"Subject. I changed it before the urge to dent your skull overwhelmed me." Butterflies had come to life in my stomach. The thought of having to mingle with the rich and powerful for hours was too much. I hoped I didn't trip and face plant in front of everyone. Wait, if I did, I could duck out early.

A glance at Thorandryll changed my mind. He wouldn't let me leave because of a little embarrassment.

"She'll be pleased to see you again."

"Who?"

"Queen Maeve." He frowned. "You seem unusually scatterbrained tonight."

"Yeah, sorry."

"Are you nervous?"

"Nope." Hell yes. "I'm good."

Up went his left eyebrow. "You're lying."

"Okay, maybe a little nervous. This isn't my usual scene." And he was so not the guy I wanted to go to a party with. Not that I often wanted to go to parties. Especially not this one.

"You're welcome to spend the evening mostly silent and gazing in adoration at me."

My eyes tried to roll right out of their sockets. "Keep dreaming, elf boy."

"This may be a shock for you, but there are several women who'd love to be on my arm tonight."

"Too bad I'm not one of them, huh?"

"Yes, it is. We'd both be more comfortable." He smiled, and drained his glass. Perfect timing, because the limo stopped, and someone opened the door.

Thorandryll slid out like a greased eel, bending to look at me while holding out his hand. Come along, Discordia."

Vaguely aware there were a lot of people outside, I concentrated on not having a wardrobe malfunction while leaving the car.

"Smile," he murmured while pulling me upright. I did, and he stepped aside and turned, tucking my hand over his forearm.

Roughly a dozen flashes blinded me, and my smile froze.

The press was here.

I was going to kill him. Very, very soon.

Somehow, I made it through the walk to his mansion, and the frequent stops for photos, without losing my smile. A servant took my coat just inside the doors, and I let the smile go, shooting Thorandryll the dirtiest look in my arsenal. "You're dead."

"Come along." He was still smiling, with a definite smugness.

"His Highness, Prince Thorandryll, and Lady Discordia Jones," a booming voice announced the second we reached the ballroom entrance.

I had no choice about the halt to let everyone see us, because Thorandryll stopped to scan the crowd inside. Every pair of eyes in the huge room turned our way. I whispered through my hastily donned smile and clenched teeth, "We can move now."

He ignored me, continuing to look about the huge room. I wondered what it felt like, to throw a party that brought everyone who was anyone running.

I spotted Mr. Whitehaven, my fake smile turning genuine at the stern expression my boss wore. His eyes were faintly glowing, just enough that I knew they were more red than brown at the moment.

"You're in so much trouble with my boss," I whispered.

"I'm hardly at fault for his failure to realize this would be a newsworthy event."

"Keep telling yourself that, buddy." Maybe Whitehaven would strangle the prince for me.

Thorandryll decided to stop playing lord of all he surveyed, and down the steps we went. A surge of people met us at the bottom, all of them eager to greet the host.

I stood there like a bump on a log, smiling and nodding as he introduced me to people whose names I forgot a few seconds after hearing them. My grip on Thorandryll's arm slowly tightened, due to a growing feeling of suffocation.

Apparently, Thorandryll noticed, or maybe I'd clamped down hard enough to inhibit his circulation, because he began to walk forward. People who'd been greeted fell away, replaced with new faces.

I gave silent thanks to Sal for his advice on improving my mental shield. Without it, the giddy excitement of those around us would've dropped me to the floor in a hysterically laughing heap.

We came face to face with the Rex, Ryan O'Meara. A lovely, statuesque woman with warm, dark brown skin was on his arm, and his sons flanked them. The atmosphere changed, as though people were holding their breath, waiting to see what would happen.

Me, I grinned, happy to see familiar faces, even if Tanner's face wasn't a friendly one. "Hello, Mr. O'Meara. Hi, Connor."

"Miss Jones, so very good to see you. My wife, Hadiya."

She extended her fine-boned hand, her golden-brown eyes warm. "At last we meet."

I remembered not to man-shake her hand. "Very pleased. I love your name."

Hadiya smiled. "I quite like yours, as well."

"Thank you."

Connor edged forward, sticking his hand out, so I switched to him. His gentle tug made me lean toward him, and he kissed my cheek.

Thorandryll suddenly remembered his manners, and greeted the Rex, while extending his hand. They shook, and the elf executed a sort of half bow over Hadiya's hand as he pretended to kiss her fingers.

He didn't make contact, but we were the only ones close enough to know. The appearance was enough, one of Thorandyll's "useful illusions" he seemed so fond of.

The atmosphere lightened, and I almost looked around to see if his gesture had lit fire to gossiping. But the lions were taking their leave, and my clan members were right behind them.

Terra looked positively radiant in her golden gown, a bright spark of life next to Dane's somber black tie. At only eighteen, she was handling the situation like a pro, her expression serene as she extended her hand to Thorandryll. "Your Highness."

"Welcome, your Majesty." He repeated his faux hand kiss—dude really was all about the illusions—while I winked at Dane before looking at Logan.

My future dating partner smiled, and I shivered. He looked fabulously dashing in black tie. Caught up in staring at him, it took me a full two seconds to realize Moira wasn't on his arm.

Instead, Danielle stood beside him, looking sophisticated and dangerous in a sleek black dress. She offered a toothy smile framed with blood red lips.

Surprised, I 'pathed Logan. *Where's Moira?*

She decided the crowd would be too much, he sent back. *Danielle was the only other one who had a fancy dress.*

I nearly missed my cue as Terra turned to me, but managed to catch her hand, and we traded air kisses to keep from leaving lip prints on each other's cheeks. The contact informed me that her assured mask was also all about appearances.

She was vibrating with excitement. I squeezed her hand before letting go. With a rustle of gauze and silk, Terra moved to the side, allowing Logan and Danielle to step forward. "You've met my Protector."

"Yes," Thorandryll replied. His arm bumped mine as he prepared to shake hands with Logan.

Logan ignored him, reaching forward for my hand, and neatly executed a bow before pressing his warm lips to my knuckles.

He smiled while straightening, catching Thorandryll off guard by immediately offering to shake, and a casual, "Thanks for the invitation."

"You're quite welcome," Thorandryll coolly replied as they finished their handshake. He seemed ready to walk off, but I stuck my hand out to Danielle.

"Love your dress, it really suits you."

Surprise slackened her face, but she quickly rallied. "Thank you. Yours is lovely as well."

"Thanks." We skipped the air kisses, which was okay by me.

Then Thorandryll excused us, sweeping me across the floor. A servant offered a tray of glasses, from which the prince selected two. Our grand entrance was over. I celebrated surviving it with a sip of champagne, its bubbles tickling my tongue.

Mr. Whitehaven appeared beside me, silent and tall. He'd chosen white tie, his long hair nearly invisible against the white tux jacket.

Thorandryll turned when I did, but stayed behind me. "Lord Whitehaven. Such an honor to have you here."

His redly glowing eyes matched the low growl of his reply. "It's proving to be an evening of surprises."

"Someone's in trouble," I softly sang before having another sip. The champagne was fantastic, its bubbles revealing different fruit flavors as they burst. This one strawberry, that one peach. One left a hint of blackberry.

My boss glanced down at me, and I grinned back, happy to know he was ready to jump down Thorandryll's throat. Mr. Whitehaven's stern expression melted into a fond smile. He bent enough to bestow a grandfatherly kiss on my forehead. "You look lovely, Discordia."

"You look smashing, boss." Or ready to start smashing, as his smile disappeared when he refocused on Thorandryll.

"We have something to discuss, sir. My office, tomorrow at ten."

"O-of course, my lord."

"Ooh, can I come too?" I really wanted to be there when the boss ripped Prince Snooty Pants a new one.

"Certainly." Mr. Whitehaven patted my shoulder and left, but not without narrowing his eyes at Thorandryll.

I giggled. "You messed up good."

"He does appear displeased."

"You think?" The champagne was going straight to my head, giving our surroundings a mellow glow. "Wow, really swanky."

The ballroom looked larger, and so did the crowd. I wasn't the only woman present who'd chosen simple over glittering when it came to a gown, which made me feel better. Of course, everyone else's "simple" probably cost four times what my ensemble had, but I decided it wasn't worth worrying about.

The floor was black and glossy, the walls white, and golden-edged niches displayed paintings or statues. Six white columns held the ceiling high above our heads. I looked up to find a mural decorating the ceiling, of elves, their beautiful white horses, and black and tan hounds rushing through a forest.

Whatever the painted figures were after wasn't visible, to my relief.

"You like it?" Thorandryll placed his hand on my back, a little too close to my rear for comfort. "It could be yours."

My laugh turned heads. "Seriously? Didn't we already agree that wasn't happening? Like, ever?"

"You made a statement to that effect. I hardly agreed," he said, his breath warm on my ear. "You should reconsider. Such a match would be quite advantageous for us both."

"Yeah, right. Hey." He'd taken my glass of champagne. "I wasn't done with that."

"We're expected to begin the dancing. I do hope you can waltz."

Crap, looked like more "center of attention" was in my immediate future.

TWELVE

By just after nine, my feet hurt and I'd lost all hope of remembering a single name that didn't belong to anyone I already knew. I was also slightly drunk from sipping champagne between turns around the floor.

Fortunately, a servant announced it was time for dinner, and the exodus from ballroom to a grand dining hall took less time than I'd have thought, with so many people.

Thorandryll's theatrics weren't limited to the ballroom. Our table, a long rectangle topped in dark green, bountifully laden with vases of flowers and gorgeous place settings, dominated the end of the hall.

All the other tables were round, and spaced comfortably apart to fill the rest of the cavernous space. The floor was green marble with glittery streaks of gold, the walls golden panels decorated with flowering vines.

No columns here. They would've blocked the view of the head table. Thorandryll seated me on his left, and I nodded at Queen Maeve, who sat to the right of his chair.

Alleryn slipped into place on my left. "Enjoying yourself?"

"You betcha. I've thought of a dozen ways to murder your prince since we arrived." I slipped my shoes off, having noted the tablecloth reached the floor in front. The cool marble felt fantastic against my poor feet. Heels weren't my usual choice for footwear.

Alleryn chuckled. "He has been flaunting you."

"'S alright, because I'm sure the boss is going to flaunt him about the head tomorrow." I leaned to look past him. "Where's Kate?"

"Seated with the rest of your friends from work."

He used his chin to indicate where I should look. Their table was halfway across the dining hall, not quite center. I checked the tables around them, to find the lions and tigers sharing one, and at another, a quad of people I vaguely remembered having been introduced to as cougars sat with Patrick, Nick, and their parents.

How had I missed running into them? I turned to Alleryn when Nick's head rose and began to turn in my direction. "What are they doing here?"

"My prince extended invitations to all the city's leaders." He gave a slight shrug. "We didn't actually think they'd all accept."

"Is he looking at me?"

"Nick? Yes."

"Great."

Thorandryll touched my forearm, and I turned to find him leaning toward me. "I'll have him ejected if his presence offends you."

"No, don't do that. Everything's cool." I could deal, to avoid Nick being embarrassed, and his father causing a scene.

"As you wish." Thorandryll stood, collecting a small golden bell, and rang it twice. Conversations stopped, leaving the hall entirely silent. "Allow me to extend my appreciation to you all for attending tonight."

I tuned out as he gave his speech, peppering it with words like "grand" and "momentous". My stomach quietly growled to inform me it wanted food, but I couldn't do anything to fulfill its request.

No big surprise that Thorandryll loved the sound of his own voice, and managed to speak for a good ten minutes before sitting down to overly enthusiastic applause.

I poked Alleryn in the ankle with my toes. "What time is it?"

"Nine-twenty-three."

"Argh."

He chuckled. "We'll eat, and return to the ballroom by eleven-thirty. Bit more dancing, drinking, and mingling before a midnight toast."

"Can I go home after that?"

"Oh, you poor dear. People won't begin to take their leave until two. No one will want to be the first, or the last, to leave."

I sighed. "I volunteer to shoulder the burden of being the first to go."

An appetizer had appeared, some sort of beautifully presented fowl. "Ooh, food."

Alleryn laughed, but I didn't care. I picked up the proper fork an instant after Thorandryll did, and tried to forget some people were slyly watching us.

"I need this recipe," I said after my first taste of the squab.

"You cook?" The question came from Maeve.

"Yes, ma'am. It's my hobby."

"Interesting." Her tone indicated cooking was beneath her, but she was Queen of the Unseelie. Probably didn't even know how to boil water. At least not on a stove.

"I'll see that you receive the recipe," Thorandryll said.

"Thanks."

Logan's calm mental voice sounded in my head. *How are you holding up?*

Better now that there's food.

Have you noticed that Nick's here?

Yeah, Thorandryll offered to kick him out. I said no.

That was a nice decision.

It's not like I hate him.

I know, Logan said before changing the subject. *Any chance you have room on your dance card later?*

I hid my smile by taking another bite. *If my feet have recovered, you're on.*

I'll pray for their recovery.

"When do you plan to make the announcement?" I heard Maeve ask.

"The negotiations aren't complete," Thorandryll answered. What were they talking about?

"It's necessary to complete them quickly."

Exasperation sharpened his reply. "She's not exactly open to the thought."

"Then make her open to it."

"Mother..."

"Or I will." The ice in her voice made me shiver. Who were they talking about? I noticed Alleryn watching me, his expression as smooth as a mannequin's.

Uh-oh. They were talking about me, weren't they? All of Thorandryll's comments tonight...was she the reason he kept harping about us becoming a couple?

Something wrong? Logan asked, startling me.

Why?

You felt scared there for a second.

I needed to pay attention to whether or not I shut down links after mental conferences with people. *Just overheard something I don't like the sound of.*

What?

Have to tell you later. Maybe if it's not too late, you could come over for coffee after this shindig?

Sure.

Okay. Talk later. This time, I made certain to cut off the link, while putting my fork down.

"Cordi?" Alleryn murmured.

"What?"

"Do you want more wine?"

A perfectly innocent question, yet I immediately wondered if he was trying to get me plastered. People had a tendency to make terrible decisions under the influence. "Actually, I'd like to switch to water."

He smiled, and lifted a hand to summon a servant. "Lady Discord would prefer water with her meal."

"Yes, my lord."

"I would too," Alleryn said, with a sly wink for me. I felt bad for suspecting him of conspiring against me. Then again, he was an elf and had been Thorandryll's healer long before I'd come into the picture.

Looking back at my plate as the servant switched our glasses, I discovered the second course had arrived. It was gazpacho, garnished with green onions and a dab of sour cream.

In sixth grade, Tina Baines had given me the unwelcome nickname of Cordi the Pig during lunch one day. I'd spent two miserable weeks "dieting" in an effort to lose the baby fat tenaciously clinging to my cheeks, stomach, and thighs.

Ginger told my mom about it, after hunger made me cranky enough to yell at her. Mom had immediately called a family council, during which both parents repeated their advice about not allowing other people's words to change my perception of my physical appearance. They'd also pointed out I hadn't even hit puberty yet, and that I'd see big changes once I did.

They'd been right, because puberty had struck the following summer, and I'd started 7th grade 6 inches taller, lean, leggy, and pretty self-conscious about two new additions that required my first real bra.

Absolute vindication for me, after the misery of 6th grade, because Tina and her clique hadn't given up their name calling. Nope, they'd tripled their efforts to shame me because I enjoyed food.

Luckily, they hadn't shamed me into an eating disorder, and I still loved food. More at that moment than ever, with a small bowl of gazpacho awaiting transfer to my stomach.

Forget scheming elves. I had a sumptuous meal ahead of me, and was going to enjoy every bite.

After that, there was an excellent possibility I'd want to meet the chef and beg for cooking lessons, judging by the first courses.

The fish course was halibut garnished with tiny flowers and pearl onions. It took all my self-control not to moan my way through it and the following courses, from the lemon-basil sorbet to the absolutely sumptuous baked meringues drizzled with a reduction of cherries, rosewater, vanilla, and topped with dark pink rose petals.

I ate every bite, busy planning a way to kidnap Thorandryll's chef, because I obviously knew jack about cooking.

The prince waited until I'd finished dessert before asking, "Was everything to your liking?"

"I really want to meet your chef," I said, wishing I had seconds of dessert. "I need to worship."

Thorandryll's smile made it clear he was about to respond with another pushy remark, and he did. "He could prepare all your meals in the future."

"Why do you have to keep bringing that up?" I leaned closer, lowering my voice. "I told you I was willing to give being your friend a shot, and would consider a public declaration of alliance. But that's it, all that's on the table."

"So you've repeatedly said, which brings to mind 'the lady doth protest too much'."

My breath huffed out. "Maybe because the man in the equation doesn't seem to comprehend the meaning of 'not gonna happen'."

"I will give you anything you desire." Thorandryll rose from his chair, and helped me out of mine. His eyebrows scrunched. "You seem shorter."

"I took off my shoes." About to duck down to grab them, I stopped when his fingers closed around my hand.

"Allow me." He went to one knee, and I tried to free myself, because damn if it didn't look like he was about to propose. Thorandryll easily kept hold, because I was trying not to make a huge scene, aware that a lot of people were watching, as they left their tables.

He gestured with his free hand, and my pumps slid out from under the table. Placing them in front of me, he smoothly stood, and caught my other hand. "There."

The pointy-eared bastard smiled. I stepped into my shoes, inching closer to him. He didn't back away. I gritted my teeth. "Thank you."

"My pleasure." For a second, I thought he was going to kiss me, but I hissed and his smile widened. He stepped back, releasing one of my hands, and gestured. "The night's not over."

"Dinner is, and that was the deal." I wanted to go home, change into my pajamas, and snuggle with my dogs. I wasn't cut out for the game-playing and the illusions of elven politics. There was no telling what people thought after all of his crap.

"I did clarify 'an evening'."

Had he? I couldn't remember the exact wording.

"Fine, but I won't need a ride home."

Thorandryll tucked my hand over his forearm to lead me away. "It'd be the height of discourtesy for me not to ensure you arrive safely at home."

"A swift kick in the family jewels is more discourteous."

He actually laughed. "Very well."

To my immense relief, Kethyrdryll stopped us at the foot of the ballroom stairs. "My apologies, brother, but my evening won't be complete unless I have the honor of a dance with Lady Discordia."

"Don't abscond with her," Thorandryll said.

"And leave you pining for the lack of her company? Of course not."

"Oh good night," I muttered. "Enough with the flowery yapping."

They turned identical boyish grins on me before Kethyrdryll offered his arm. I grabbed it as though he were offering a life line. Four steps, and we turned to face each other, our arms moving to proper waltzing position. Off we went, and he studied my face. "You're not enjoying yourself."

"Your brother's a hard-headed jerk."

Kethyrdryll laughed loudly enough that the couples dancing closest looked at us. "My apologies."

"It's not your fault, but thanks for the rescue." I hesitated. "He's really pushing for us becoming a couple."

"Thoran's never dealt with rejection well, or with failing to achieve his goals."

"I think your mother has something to do with it."

Kethyrdryll glanced back to where we'd left Thorandryll. He was busy talking to several other men. "Of course she does. Our mother believes in having every advantage possible."

"And I'd be an advantage."

He nodded. "She wants firm alliances in place to keep her kingdom secure. I dislike saying this, but it would've been better for you to have let her die."

I had to close my mouth and swallow before responding. "She's your mother."

"She's the Unseelie Queen, first and foremost. As that, she will seldom retreat from the course of action she chooses. You are not only an extremely gifted natural mage, but someone two gods appear to have an interest in. And one of them humbled her before her people."

"Oh, so her idea of revenge on Sal is to sic Thorandryll on me, and hope we'll end up married?"

"Sal ... oh, the nameless god. You haven't discovered which one he is yet?"

I shook my head. "I haven't seen him since the showdown."

Kethyrdryll grimaced. "I'll try to discover who he is, but it can be difficult. The gods enjoy confusion, and most have several faces."

"I'd really appreciate that." The music faded, a new tune beginning a few seconds later. "Can we sit this out?"

"I believe someone plans to cut in." Kethyrdryll smiled, looking past my shoulder. "Well met, Logan."

"Nice to see you again." They didn't shake hands. Instead, they did what I'd heard called a warrior's greeting, grasping each other's arm just below the elbow. "Mind if I ask her for a dance?"

"Not at all." Kethyrdryll looked at me. "We'll speak later."

"Sure. Thanks." We watched him walk away.

"So, dance card. Did you save me a spot?"

"I did, as long as you promise to scope out a hidey hole after. I need some air."

"I promise. We'll just waltz right outside before the music ends."

"Awesome."

As we began to dance, Terra and Connor whirled past, staring into each other's eyes. I remembered the vision I'd had, and smiled.

"That's only the second real smile I've seen from you tonight," Logan said.

"You're my favorite dance partner." If he hadn't noticed the way they were looking at each other, I wasn't going to point it out. Connor was a good guy, and Terra was old enough to make her own decisions.

"Good to know. It's been an interesting evening."

I laughed. "Hasn't it just? Hear any juicy gossip?"

"All the gossip's been about you, who you are, and why Thorandryll has you on his arm tonight." Logan's eyes flashed from dark to light and back.

I wrinkled my nose. "Figures."

"What was he doing, right after dinner? That really set tongues to wagging."

"I forgot to put my shoes back on."

Logan's forehead creased. "What?"

"I'm not used to walking and dancing in heels so much. I slipped them off the minute I sat down."

He chuckled. "He made quite a production out of getting them for you."

"Yeah, the bastard." I sighed. "He's been a jerk all evening."

"Our parties are better." Logan grinned, angling us toward a set of open doors I didn't remember seeing earlier. A cool breeze wafted in.

"Yes, they are. Way better. Well, except maybe the food. I want to kidnap his chef."

"That was an amazing meal," Logan agreed, snagging two glasses of champagne from a passing servant. "Okay, out we go."

"Hurray." Outside, we found a wide stone balcony overlooking a garden. Steps led down to it, and there were other couples strolling around. "Pretty."

"Chairs." He handed me a glass, nodding at the left end of the balcony.

"Chairs are good. Fantastic even." We crossed and sat down. I kicked off my shoes and propped my feet on another chair facing mine. "Bliss."

Logan stretched out to do the same, crossing his ankles. "Yes, this is better."

"Mm." I had a sip and put my glass down on the ground beside my chair. They were thickly padded, nearly as comfy as my sofa. I covered a yawn. "Oh, sorry."

"I'm tired too."

"Maybe we should forget the coffee. Alleryn said it'd be two before anyone will think of leaving."

Logan regarded me for a moment. "Up to you. It'd be a nice way to wind down, after all the noise and people."

"Hm. I could fake a tummy ache after the midnight toast."

"And I could talk Terra into leaving about then." He smiled. "O'Meara too. I don't think his queen is having a great time."

I made a face. "Too bad. She's gorgeous."

"Yes, she is, and she's also nice. The Pride has great respect for her."

I wiggled my toes. "Guess she hasn't gotten much respect tonight. I like her name. It's pretty."

"It means 'gift', and I believe that's exactly how O'Meara feels about her." Logan knocked back his champagne. "Lord Whitehaven hasn't been in a good mood."

"Blame Thorandryll. They're having a meeting tomorrow."

Logan chuckled. "Wish I could be there for it."

"I'll tell you all about it. The boss said I could go."

"I look forward to your report. So, is that our plan for escape?"

"Yes. I'll put on a good, but subdued show. Just come over once you get home."

"I'm going to change first."

"Aw, but you look fantastic in a tux." I pouted.

"Thank you, but you've apparently never worn one. Not the most comfortable clothes." He tugged at his bow tie. "Feels like I'm choking."

"Oh, all right."

THIRTEEN

We weren't allowed to relax for long. Kethyrdryll came out onto the terrace, an icy-faced Danielle on his arm. "There you are. It's only a few minutes to the hour."

I groaned. "Toast time approaches. Better put my shoes back on."

"Where's Terra?" Logan asked Danielle.

"Dancing with the Rex's younger son. Soames is keeping watch."

Kethyrdryll moved to help me stand. "I'll escort you to my brother."

"Okay. Thanks." Man, my feet were killing me. Too bad I hadn't had time to break in the new shoes before the party.

Danielle latched onto Logan's arm the second he rose, while shooting a frown at me. I couldn't exactly blame her, since I'd kind of stolen her date. They followed us back into the ballroom, but not all the way to where Thorandryll was holding court with a gaggle of mostly female admirers.

If the setting were different, Thorandryll likely would've been mobbed. I wondered if he were using glamour on them, and realized it'd been some time since I'd suffered an attack of the Hazies around him.

"There you are, my dear." Thorandryll quipped, sending a million-watt smile my way. Several of the women followed that with less-than-friendly faces.

"I'm not your dear, just your date." The last thing I needed was a bunch of women out for my blood. My feet hurt too much to run.

His smile dimmed, but Thorandryll gave a slight shake of his head. "Your poor self-esteem hinders you."

"Your arrogance blinds you." I smiled, noticing not a single woman was paying any attention to Kethyrdryll. Why not? The two of them looked exactly alike, aside from eye color. Did the title of Prince really make that much of a difference to people? "You should work on that."

Thorandryll laughed, moving through his admirers to take my arm. Kethyrdryll stepped back to collect two glasses of champagne from a waiting servant. He handed them to us, took one for himself, and disappeared into the crowd.

With a bow to the ladies, the prince led me toward the stairs. "We discussed appearances."

"Believe me, I'm being nice. If I weren't there would be yelling." I gritted my teeth as we began climbing the steps. "My feet hurt and my stomach's unhappy."

"I thought you enjoyed the meal."

"Yeah, but not all the damn attention. I'm going home after the toast."

"The party won't end for ..."

"See my face? It's the face of someone who has had enough. My 'enough face' is followed quickly by my cranky face." We'd reached the top of the stairs. "Cranky face is one you don't want to see."

"Very well. I'll escort you out after the toast, so that you may teleport home." He was smiling instead of looking irritated. Why did my insistence on leaving make him happy?

As we turned to face the ballroom, I saw the number of women staring at him. Oh. With me gone, he could take his pick. Fine by me.

"Friends, old and new, if I may have your attention?" Thorandryll's voice cut through the noise, attentive silence following.

He launched into another speech about his hopes for a bright future, blah, blah, blah, and I tuned him out. All I wanted to do was clink, sip, and get the hell out of there.

Without more media attention.

A deep gonging signaled the end of Thorandryll's wordy toast, and he lifted his glass. I followed suit before he touched his glass to mine. The ballroom resounded with others doing the same and everyone had the obligatory sip before the crowd noise resumed.

"Okay. I'm out."

"A moment." He looked around, still smiling, and finally nodded. "Alright."

When I turned, Thorandryll slid his arm around my waist. I stepped clear once we were in the hallway and handed him my glass. "Thanks for the dinner. See you in the morning."

Satisfaction made me smile when my reminder caused him to wince. I teleported home.

It was after one before Logan knocked on my front door. "Come in. Coffee's ready."

"Wonderful." We traded a cheek rub, and headed for the kitchen.

After pouring coffee I said, "That was an interesting evening."

"Yeah. Terra had a good time."

"Any trouble?" I took a sip and watched his face.

"No, which I guess shouldn't surprise me. Thorandryll wouldn't want his party tainted."

"Of course not. I'm pretty sure he's in big trouble with Mr. Whitehaven. That's got to be enough for anyone, right?"

Logan nodded. "Absolutely. What was it you heard, during dinner?"

"Elves being their usual, conniving selves. I think Maeve is behind Thorandryll's sudden marrying fever."

"His what?"

Oh, right. I hadn't mentioned that to him. "He thinks we need an official alliance. Told me the best option was for us to marry."

Logan's eyes began to lighten. "Really."

"Yup. I told him where he could stuff that idea."

"I bet you did."

"So then, he said a regular alliance would work. I told him I needed to discuss that with Terra." I grinned. "Not that I'm in a hurry to, after tonight."

He smiled back. "Good."

It was time for a subject change. "Any idea when you're going to talk to the boss?"

"This week."

"Cool. It'll be a lot of fun, all of us working together." And I'd be able to see him nearly every day, without worrying about Danielle's hovering disapproval.

"Are you certain it won't be a problem, with us dating?" Logan's eyes were dark green again.

I shook my head. "I think we can handle both better than Nick and I did. You're not all pushy and possessive."

"Well, damn. I was going to ask when we could have another date."

My laugh put a smile on his face. "That's not pushy. We're dating now. It's expected. How about next Friday, work permitting?"

"It's a date." He finished his coffee. "I should go. You have a meeting in the morning."

"I do." Placing my coffee cup on the counter, I said, "Promise I'll share the juicy details."

"I can't wait. Walk me out?"

I did and reveled in the hug and kiss we shared before he said, "Good night."

"Night." After shutting and locking the front door, I leaned against it, still smiling.

Dating Logan was definitely not a bad idea. In fact, it might be one of my best ideas ever.

FOURTEEN

At 9:45 AM, I teleported to the office, meeting Mr. Whitehaven as he unlocked the doors. The elves hadn't arrived yet, and since we were closed for New Year's Day, Tabitha wasn't there. It was my chance to cross one of my questions off my list. "Good morning, boss."

"Good morning." He pushed the door and held it open for me.

"I've been meaning to ask you something," I said while walking inside.

He followed me in. "Yes?"

"I found out there's a dragon living in Santo Trueno." I turned around to look at him. "Are you the dragon?"

Mr. Whitehaven smiled. "Why would you think I'm the dragon?"

"Your eyes glow red sometimes, and I know you've been around for a really long time. Everyone tacks 'Lord' on you, and they all say you're an important person in the supe community." I held up my forefinger. "And you keep treasures in your office."

"Good points, all quite logical. However, I am not the dragon, though I am closely affiliated with him."

"How close?"

My boss was still smiling. "I am his plenipotentiary."

"His what?"

"It means, that for all intents and purposes, I am the dragon. He usually prefers not to deal with others, so I handle matters for him as a stand in."

"Oh." That was a little confusing. "But you're not actually him."

"No."

"If you're not the dragon, what are you?"

Mr. Whitehaven's smile faded slightly. "A hybrid. The dragon is my father, and my mother was human. I cannot take full dragon shape."

Processing his words took a moment. I took that moment before asking, "But you can change your shape?"

"Yes, to a degree." He didn't appear willing to add any specifics. I decided I'd been nosey enough.

"Cool. I've been curious since we met, but wanted to try and figure it out for myself."

Mr. Whitehaven nodded. "You were close."

Beyond him, I saw a limo turn into the parking lot. "Thorandryll's here. Want me to make coffee?"

"No, thank you, unless you wish to have some. I'm not interested in offering that much hospitality this morning."

My chortle of delight refreshed his smile.

Thorandryll had brought his mommy, Queen Maeve of the Unseelie. Coward.

A man, dressed in gray jeans and a faded Pink Floyd tee, had followed them in, but I wasn't sure he was with them. No one objected to his presence. I kept my mouth closed and curiosity in check, expecting Mr. Whitehaven to make introductions once we'd settled in his office.

The two elves chose the sofa. I sat in one of the chairs on the right side of the office, and the stranger perched on the corner of Whitehaven's desk.

My boss didn't disappoint me. "Discordia, this is Lord Kadon. Lord Kadon, Miss Discordia Jones."

We nodded to each other. He appeared to be mid-twenties or so, with medium brown hair and gray eyes. His skin was lightly tanned. The "Lord" looked like any twenty-something who spent his days hanging out at a music store or comic book shop.

Mr. Whitehaven focused on Thorandryll. "I'm quite displeased with the public display you created last night."

"Such a grand social occasion always attracts the media, my lord," Thorandryll said.

"Yeah, well, you could've told me, and I would've teleported. Instead, you paraded me in front of all the cameras." I leaned back in my seat, crossing my arms to glare at the prince. "I don't want to be in the spotlight. Do you have any idea how hard it's going to be for me to do any undercover work for a while?"

"My son showed you great favor last night. He could have had the companionship of anyone, yet he chose you." Queen Maeve waved her hand at me, forestalling any protest I might make, and concentrated on the two Lords at the desk. "She must grow accustomed to such attention. It will become commonplace once she and Thorandryll marry."

I nearly choked, spluttering in my haste to respond to that. "I'm not marrying him."

May as well have kept my mouth shut, for all the attention she paid to me. Maeve continued, her voice level and clear. "It's the best solution to the problem."

"What problem?"

That got her attention. "You. We simply cannot allow someone such as you to run amok, upsetting the balance of things with your displays of power and ignorance."

"Excuse me?" What the hell was she talking about? At a complete loss, I looked at my boss.

"Discordia has the right to determine her own place in the world. You have no authority to command her." Mr. Whitehaven's eyes began to glow.

If Maeve were intimidated, she didn't show it. "You do."

"I wouldn't dream of meddling in her in personal life."

A chuckle from Thorandryll turned all eyes his way. "No? Yet you hire shifters to work with her."

"What the hell does that have to do with anything?" I asked, a little louder than I meant to be. "And just why the hell am I some big problem?"

Lord Kadon chose to answer my questions. "You, my dear, are considered a problem by some, because you walk the line between humanity and the rest of us. You are one of us, due to the power you've inherited, yet not because you weren't born in our realm. Your morals are human, therefore there are many who are uncomfortable with where your loyalties may fall."

"It's not like I'm the only psychic in the world. There's thousands of us." Where my loyalty may fall in regards to what? I pointed at Thorandryll. "And I am not marrying him."

"You must." Maeve glared at me. "You're too chaotic. You must be controlled, so that your actions don't impact the fragile peace we currently enjoy."

Something tempered my immediate reaction, so that I responded to her far more calmly than intended. "Really? I saved your life, instead of Rhaetha's, the woman you threw into your dungeon and left to the mercy of the very god who'd driven her crazy. Was that a bad decision that caused chaos, or a good one that prevented it?"

Before she could say anything, I kept going. "I've helped in keeping demons from taking over this city, and oh, Dalsarin the dark elf and his cranky pants god from doing that too. Where those bad decisions that caused chaos?"

"Of course they weren't." Thorandryll scooted forward on the sofa, after a glance at his mother. Resting his elbows on his knees, he looked at me. "For someone so young, and newly come into her power, you've done much good. But power corrupts, Miss Jones, and humans have become more susceptible to such corruption since the Sundering."

"Oh, and I guess elves aren't susceptible to corruption. I mean, it's not like you guys think you can just order people around or anything. Or think that you know it all, and the rest of us are idiots who can't figure out how to tie our shoes." I scowled. "I'll tell you something right now: You're not the boss of me. You don't get to tell me what to do, when to do it, how to do it, or whom to do it with. Not even he," I jabbed my forefinger at Mr. Whitehaven. "Gets to tell me what to do past normal operations here at Arcane Solutions."

"You don't understand." Maeve's eyes were flashing.

"I understand the only chaos I've caused is having anything to do with elves who think they need to 'control' me, and tell me what to do with my own damn life. And what the hell does my working with shifters have to with anything?"

"They are a lesser species, one you've too closely aligned yourself with. A lesser species that should be destroyed."

"Try it, and you'll find out exactly how much chaos I can cause, lady," I said at the same time Thorandryll spoke.

"Mother, that won't help the situation."

"I think you're a bunch of elitist pricks, looking down on shifters the way you do. Who gives a flip if they started out as regular animals? That was ages ago. They evolved. That's what nearly everything does: evolve."

Thorandryll threw up his hands and leaned back, a mulish frown on his face. "I told you not to broach that subject, Mother."

Maeve ignored him. "You're exactly like your ancestors, girl. Arrogant, yet you lower yourself to the mud by playing with animals."

"Yeah? You can go screw your..."

"Enough." Lord Kadon didn't shout the word, but it closed both our mouths. I was sort of glad he'd broken in, because I felt flushed and sweaty, and could feel my pyrokinesis boiling behind the door of its room in my mental maze. "I believe that Miss Jones has made herself very clear. She will not consider marrying your son, or otherwise place herself under your control, Maeve."

Interesting how he used her first name, and only it.

The Unseelie Queen rose to her feet. "I believe that's a decision you and she both will come to regret."

With that, she stalked out of Mr. Whitehaven's office. Thorandryll stood, hesitated long enough to make a half-bow toward the two men, and followed her out. We heard the glass doors swing shut behind them.

I looked at my boss. "What did she mean by 'fragile peace'? Why is she so gung ho that I need to be controlled?"

My boss's eyes were no longer glowing, and there was a smug twist to his lips. "Our acceptance by humans is a delicately balanced matter, Discordia. They have their science, their weapons, and their greater numbers, while we have magic and certain other advantages. Though it appears relatively calm on the surface, the fear that began when the Melding occurred is still present."

I remembered my thought about how easy it would be to bomb the Barrows, and be rid of vampires in the city. "She thinks World War III is gonna break out?"

"Her worry isn't far-fetched," Lord Kadon said, picking at a frayed spot on the thigh of his gray jeans. "We have two factions, both consisting of humans and supernaturals: Those who believe we can peacefully co-exist, and those who do not."

"Guessing the now absent Queen is in Camp Two." Possibly the Mayor was too, which certainly didn't make them allies. My skin had cooled, and my pyrokinesis ability was quiet again. "But my marrying Thorandryll wouldn't change jack, if the elves started something."

"It would, because you'd be under constant surveillance, and therefore, easy to imprison to keep you from acting."

A chill raised the hair at the nape of my neck, and goosebumps broke out on my arms. "How many people think the same way she does?"

"Enough that it's an issue, particularly here in this city." Mr. Whitehaven shook his head. "But it's not confined to supernaturals. There are humans who believe as she does."

"You were raised human. What lengths will humanity go to, in order to remain the rulers of the world?" Kadon looked at me, and my mouth went dry. He nodded without waiting for me to answer. "Exactly. Let's shelve this unpleasant matter, and move onto something I can help with."

I stared at him. "What?"

"You've a curse hanging over you."

Who and what the hell was...I looked from him to my boss, and back again. "You're the dragon, aren't you? That's why she didn't argue with you."

Lord Kadon smiled. "I am."

Wow. Of all the questions I could've asked, the one I did was, "Why do you look younger than your son?"

"I prefer to blend in."

"And I have found it useful to appear older," my boss added.

"People pay more attention to maturity."

He nodded. "Yes, or at least the appearance of it."

"Cool." I felt overloaded with information now, and kind of wanted to be alone to process it all. I had plans to join the family for a New Year's Eve meal at one, and now wondered if it'd be better for them if I cut ties. Better as in safer. Without thinking, I asked, "Why me?"

The two men smiled, but Kadon responded. "A fault of birth and ancestry. That's all any of us are, Miss Jones. Beings born into circumstances we seldom would choose, if given the opportunity. What we each must do is make the best of it."

Chance, in other words. "Awesome."

He slid off the desk, and gestured. "If you'll be so kind as to rise and come stand before me, I'll remove the curse from you."

"You can do that?" I was already getting out of my chair.

"Yes." When I halted in front of him, I realized he was my height. Not exactly the most impressive human male façade for a dragon. He looked me in the eye. "Don't move. I will not harm you."

"Okay." I flinched as his hands shimmered, the skin covering with iridescent white scales, and claws shooting from the ends of his fingers. "Maybe I'd better close my eyes."

"If you feel more comfortable that way."

I did, and felt the air move as he began slashing around me. The dragon slashed from the top of my head down to my feet, leaving no gaps. He even had me lift each foot. "All right, the curse is gone."

Opening my eyes, I said, "Thank you."

"You're welcome. You'll still need to find the one who cursed you. It's likely he or she will do so again."

"Right." I narrowed my eyes. "Maybe it was Maeve?"

Kadon shook his head. "No, the curse didn't react to her presence. It would've...leaned toward her, if she were its creator."

"Oh." I'd learned a few too many new things today, but at least that one was comforting.

FIFTEEN

I teleported home, feeling as though the weight of the world were on my shoulders. Not quite up to the dogs' usual exuberant welcome home, I targeted the drive in front of the garage as my landing place.

Logan was on my porch, bending down in front of my door. I said, "Hey."

He shot upright, turning wide eyes my way, and quickly relaxed. "Hey, I uh," he lifted a bunch of flowers into view over the porch railing. "Brought these for you."

They were Blue Girl tea roses, actually lavender in color in spite of their name. I smiled, walking across the grass to the steps, and he met me at the bottom of them. Taking the roses, I buried my nose into their velvety petals to inhale their fruity fragrance before hugging him. "Thank you. I really kind of needed them."

"You're welcome. Do you need more of them?"

I laughed, resting my cheek against his shoulder, face turned away from his so I could sniff the roses again. "Nope, they and the hug are enough. I already feel better."

Logan began to rub my upper back with one hand, his other hand flat across my lower back. "Why did you feel bad? Too much champagne last night?"

"No, something else, but kind of Thorandryll related."

"Need to talk about it?"

I lifted my head and leaned back enough to look at his face. "Don't know. It might scare you away. Certainly scares me."

"I'm not sure anything can scare me away from you."

"Oh, my God. You just proved it: You are taking classes in how to say the exact right thing." I kissed him before pulling free, and grabbed his hand to make certain he followed me up the stairs. We sat down at the top of them, and Logan put his arm around me. I held the rose bouquet in my lap.

"No, you just bring out the best in me."

"Yeah, right." My scoffing earned a grin from him.

"We're sitting, which I take to mean you do want to talk about it. Am I right?"

I hesitated before nodding. "The meeting didn't exactly go as planned."

"Thorandryll's still in one piece? Damn." Logan gave me a little squeeze. "So how did it go?"

After I told him, Logan was silent for a moment. He didn't put any space between us, which I took as a good sign. "Lord Kadon's right. Making the best of things is all anyone can do."

"I guess, but geeze, I feel like I have a big, red bull's eye painted on my back. Like just being around me makes life more dangerous for everyone else." I bit my lip before adding, "I was thinking maybe I should stop seeing my family so much. I've already caused them enough trouble."

Logan shook his head. "I think you'd better talk to them, and let them decide."

"Mom and Dad won't like the idea."

"Right, and why should they? They love you."

I sighed, a long exhalation that seemed to come all the way from my toes. "I love them too, or I wouldn't even worry about it. And maybe I should leave the clan. You can throw me out or whatever it takes."

"No."

I turned to look at him. He was looking back. "Maeve wants shifters dead. All shifters. She doesn't like..."

"Who the hell cares what she likes? I don't. Terra doesn't. I'm damn sure O'Meara and the other shifter leaders don't either." Logan's eyes began to lighten. "Much as the elves would like to think otherwise, they are not our leaders. They aren't the leaders of anything but themselves, and maybe a few species that prefer to look to them for guidance. They've held themselves up to humans as our overlords, and they've always considered just about everyone else beneath them, but they aren't in charge."

Whew, I seemed to have struck a nerve. "Okay, then who is in charge?"

"The closest thing the supe community here has to a single leader is Lord Kadon. When he chooses to become involved, which he seldom does." Logan's eyes began to darken again. "Aside from him, it's the Council."

"The vampire Council?"

"No, the High Council, made up from chosen leaders. None of which are shifters." Logan's top lip curled a touch. "We're not considered important enough for seats on it."

That was just wrong, but figuring he already knew that, I didn't say it. "So do shifters have a Council of their own?"

"No." He suddenly grinned. "It's a cat and dog thing."

"Oh, for crying out loud." I lifted the roses for a long, deep breath of their perfume. "That's ridiculous."

He shrugged. "The wolves consider themselves better than the other canid shifters, and all canid shifters think they're better than feline shifters. That general feeling's mutual, because the canids are more prone to act on emotion."

"You're saying they're hot-headed, like me."

"You're not nearly as reactive as wolves can be," he said, squeezing me again.

"Speaking of reactive, I'm having lunch with the family today. Want to come with? There'll be plenty of food."

Logan accepted my subject change without pause. "Love to, if you're sure it's okay. I know Betty's not particularly fond of supes."

"No, but she's getting better about it." My step-mother hadn't twigged to the fact that it was my fault Dalsarin had targeted my little brother, Sean, a couple of months ago.

I hoped Betty never realized that, because our relationship had improved immensely since I'd saved Sean. Now, she was genuinely pleased to see me, instead of pretending she was for my dad's sake.

Honestly, I couldn't believe she hadn't figured it out. Maybe Betty had, but preferred to focus on the positive part of the situation: The part where I'd been willing to risk my own life for Sean's.

If that was the case, it worked for me. I'd never enjoyed making her uncomfortable.

"Then I'm game," Logan said.

"Great. Let me get the dogs."

He laughed. "They're invited too?"

"Yeah. They're family." I pecked him on the cheek before standing.

I teleported us to Mom's back yard, and braced myself as my little brothers saw us appear.

"Cordi!" both yelled, racing toward me.

Dropping to my knees, I caught them and laughed. "Hey, how are you guys?"

They didn't have a chance to answer because Amadeus, their Cocker Spaniel, began screaming in terror.

Mom, Dad, and Betty rushed out of the back door in response, Dad grabbed Amadeus, and the Spaniel peed on him. "Oh, great. That's just..." Dad held the dog clear, looking down at his clothes. "What's wrong with him?"

"He's scared of us," Bone said. *"What a wimp."*

"Be nice." I climbed to my feet. "He's scared of my big dogs."

Meanwhile Amadeus was struggling, his back legs kicking wildly. His yelping was incoherent. "Crap. Leglin, can you..."

Squishy barked. *"Stop that."*

To my surprise, Amadeus fell silent.

"They're not mean. We live with them," my chubby Chihuahua said. *"And we're littler than you."*

"I think you can put him down now."

"Good." Dad carefully put Amadeus on the ground. The Spaniel cowered at his feet, shivering violently. "Poor boy."

Prejudice even in the Animal Kingdom. How wonderful. "Let me try talking to him."

"You do that. I'm going to clean up." Dad gestured at his shirt and slacks. "Hello, Logan."

"Hi. Sorry for the noisy arrival."

My dad laughed. "Never a dull moment."

"We'd better get back to the food. I'm glad you could join us, Logan." Mom stooped to pat Amadeus. "It's alright, boy."

"It's nice to see you again." Betty smiled, her eyes flicking from Logan to my pitties. "Are you sure everything will be okay?"

Sean chose that moment to tackle Diablo. My black pit fell over sideways, grunting as Sean landed on him. Betty's face went white. Diablo turned his head and swiped his tongue across my brother's face, reducing Sean to giggles.

I smiled. "Yeah, everything will be fine. Bone and Diablo won't hurt anyone."

"Okay." Betty nibbled her bottom lip, but went inside. Pleased she was trusting me, I walked over to the furry heap that was Amadeus.

"Hey, they won't hurt you. I promise."

Amadeus lifted his head, his big, brown eyes sad. "*I can't save my kids if they attack them.*"

Aww, the poor thing. I crouched beside him. "They won't hurt the boys either. Look."

Bone was allowing Jonah to climb all over him, while Diablo had Sean pinned and was washing his face, while my brother giggled and wiggled. "See? They're good boys, like you."

The Spaniel shivered. "*They've fought.*"

"Yeah, they had to. They don't anymore, except to protect people." I stroked his back. "They'll help you protect the kids, if they're around and something happens."

"*Really?*"

"Really. Come on, I'll introduce you to them." Fortunately, that went well and no more pee fountains occurred.

"You made front page news." Mom brandished a newspaper as Logan and I walked in. "Did you have fun?"

"The food was fantastic, but I could've done without the rest. Need any help?"

"Just carrying things to the table. Logan, will you please call in the boys? Everyone needs to wash their hands." My mother was in full Mom Mode, tossing the newspaper onto the kitchen table and nodding to Betty as the latter passed her with a platter of ham.

"Yes, ma'am." Logan about-faced and went back out. Amusing how he already knew who was in charge during Jones family gatherings.

Twenty minutes later, we were all seated at the dining table. I notice the bottle of non-alcoholic, sparkling grape juice, and smiled. Mom never let kids feel left out.

"Everything looks and smells great. Thanks, Mom and Betty."

Both women smiled from their seats on either side of Dad, who sat at the head of the table. Jonah sat between Betty and me; Sean between Mom and Logan. The dogs were sitting around or under the table, licking their chops with hopeful expressions.

"Far cry from a fancy ball." Mom began filling Sean's plate.

"I think we both prefer this." Logan glanced across the table at me. "Right?"

"You bet. I know everyone, and cameras aren't being shoved in my face." I took the ham platter when Betty passed it, speared a slice, and handed the platter to Logan.

"Well, you looked lovely." Betty rose to pour wine and sparkling grape juice for everyone. "Where'd you find that dress?"

"The mall, at uh, one of the boutiques. Can't remember which one." To my dismay, Thorandryll's ball remained a big part of the dinner conversation.

Damn elf.

"No, that's enough. Their tummies are going to pop," I said, stopping Jonah from giving Speck another piece of ham. Mom had cooked two, one without glaze for the dogs.

The menfolk had fed them while Mom, Betty, and I cleaned up the kitchen.

Amadeus had recovered fully, and stood between Bone and Diablo, wiggling as they waited for more ham.

I put away the last dish. "All done. We'd better head home. I have work tomorrow."

"Alright." Mom dried her hands and hugged me. More hugs followed, as well as untangling little boys from dogs.

I teleported us home, to my front yard.

"Potty time, guys. Get to it."

Logan tugged on my hand, and I turned into him for a hug. "That was fun. I like your family."

"Thanks. Sorry about Amadeus' freak-out."

He chuckled. "He did alright. I felt sorry for him."

"Yeah. He's sort of dopey, but he loves the boys."

"Good. I," Logan kissed the tip of my nose. "Should go home. Got a few things to wrap up before I talk to Lord Whitehaven."

Darn. "Okay. I'll talk to you tomorrow."

"I'll be waiting." He dipped his head, brushing his cheek against mine, and then kissed me. "Bye."

"Bye." I felt a bit breathless, and a whole lot giddy. Was I falling in love? Watching Logan walk down the drive, I thought maybe so.

And, strangely, felt absolutely okay with it.

SIXTEEN

The next morning, Dane showed up and we decided to go have another look at where our one clue had led to.

Returning to the alley the thread had ended in didn't turn up anything new. We walked around that spot for a minute or two before Dane said, "What about widening our search? Walk a few blocks around this point?"

"Sure. If we split up, we can cover ground faster." The day was bright, no wind blowing, which made it feel warmer than the past few days.

He held up his phone. "Okay. Let me know if you find anything, and I'll do the same."

"Cool. I'll go west."

We walked back between the buildings to the street before taking off in separate directions. I covered two blocks, circling around into the alleys, and was halfway down the third when the feeling of being watched hit me.

I stopped to look around. The area had enough vehicle and foot traffic that I didn't feel as though I stuck out. If someone were watching me, I didn't want them to think I'd be easy to sneak up on.

The block was populated with small shops selling things like pottery and other local, handmade items. Two shop fronts behind me, I saw Danielle and sighed.

Danielle was tall and slender, with a face made for modeling. Her beef with me was over Logan. Alanna had told me that Danielle wanted him, and well, that wasn't working out for Danielle.

She began walking toward me. I waited, not wanting her to think I was afraid, and she halted a few feet away. "What are you doing here?"

I'd promised Logan and Terra to behave toward her, so didn't respond with a smart-ass remark. "Working a case."

Danielle flicked her long, glossy black hair off her shoulder while looking around. "Where's Soames?"

"We split up to cover more ground."

Her upper lip curled. "He's supposed to guard you."

"Broad daylight, busy shopping area. I think I can survive an hour on my own here." I didn't ask why she was there. For all I knew, she worked in the frame shop she'd apparently walked out of. "Have to get back to work."

When I turned and began to walk, Danielle took a few quick steps and stayed beside me. She was frowning when I glanced at her face. "Did you want something?"

"Our Queen has made it clear we are to protect you."

I had to give her points for her devotion to Queen and clan, but really didn't want her tagging along. "I appreciate that, but..."

"What are you looking for?"

Forget it. I wasn't going to ruin my nice day by arguing with her. "A mirror."

"Why aren't you looking in the shops? Some have mirrors for sale."

"It's a magic mirror." She did have a point, but would someone or something that could manipulate shadows turn around and hide the mirror in plain sight in a human's shop?

Danielle's frown deepened, but she didn't say anything else until we'd made the turn at the end of the block, and I entered the alley. "Really?"

"What can I say? It's not a pretty job, and alleys are part of it sometimes."

She followed me, stepping carefully to avoid flattened trash. The alleys here were in pretty decent shape, and actually paved. I didn't bother stepping on or around any bits of trash, because it was all paper or cardboard.

Near the end of the alley, I stopped as a thread appeared. "I have a trail."

It was the same dark gray color as the previous thread. Danielle stayed on my heels as I broke into a jog, following it.

Good thing, since at the end of the thread, the ground wasn't solid. It was still there, I even saw the cement and dirt layers as I dropped through it. Something slowed the fall, so I landed on my feet. Before I could look around, I had to jump to one side to keep from being flattened by Danielle.

She wasn't happy, if the scowl on her face was any indication. I pretended not to notice in favor of looking around. We were in a round tunnel, the stone walls reddish brown. I planted my hands on my hips. "Okay, we fell down a rabbit hole, but to where?"

"Obviously into a trap." Danielle sniffed the air. "But who was it set for?"

I wondered if she smelled anything useful. All I could smell was the damp dirt odor I associated with caves. Fitting, since we were basically in a cave. "Going to go with 'no one in particular,' because, seriously, who uses alleys as a regular travel way?"

"The homeless, dealers, prostitutes, and everyone who takes out their trash," Danielle said.

Duh. "Right, but that doesn't mean it's a trap set for a specific person. Maybe for specific types of people, but who would want to capture those types, and why?"

"Frankly, I don't give a damn about anything but getting out of here, so," she held out her hand. "Teleport us."

I sighed, but took hold. Once back at the spot, I'd call the office for backup, and stand guard until someone who could disarm the trap arrived. "Okay."

Fire blazed through my mind when I tried, dropping me to my knees and forcing me to release her hand. "Ow, oh crap, that hurts!"

"What happened?"

I looked up, holding my head with both hands. "I know where we are. We're in the demon realm."

Danielle's eyes widened. "We're dead."

"Oh ye of little faith. Remember, one of my roommates is an elf hound." I rubbed my temples.

"Then call him. He obeys you." Her lips turned down. "Everyone does."

"No, they don't." I managed to climb to my feet.

Danielle's laugh was too soft to echo. "Really? The entire clan kowtows to you, the great human psychic who gave us a territory to call our own."

"No one 'kowtows' to me. And I didn't give it to the clan. Logan did. I was just." I hesitated. "Just a means of making it possible."

"Exactly. If you'd never met the Protector..."

"Wait, I need to say something, okay? I'm really sorry we started off on the wrong foot. But I didn't stalk Logan in order to meet him or anything. I didn't even know the clan existed then. It was," about to say "pure chance" I didn't. Instead, I asked, "Do you ever feel like someone's messing with you? I mean, like you're a game piece on somebody's board game that they're moving around to suit themselves?"

She gazed at me, her bitter expression softening. "Is that how you feel?"

"Lately, yeah. A lot. I mean, holy crap, look at all of the things that have happened, and how many alliances I've...well, blundered into. I didn't plan any of this, it all just happened. Seriously, who does stuff like that ever 'just happen' to?"

"You're someone's pawn."

Scowling, I nodded. "Looks that way, and I don't like it."

For a moment, we were silent. Danielle shook her head. "My apologies."

"For what?"

"For the way I've behaved toward you."

"Oh. Accepted, and I'm..."

"Accepted," she said before I could finish. "Now, you were going to call your hound?"

"Right. Leglin."

My hound appeared, his inquisitive expression becoming an ear-flattened, silent snarl, after a good sniff of the air. "*This is the demon realm.*"

"We know. That's why I called you. We need a lift out."

"*Of course.*" He shook out his raised hackles, his ears flapping, and moved to my side.

I waved Danielle over. "Hold onto his collar."

She did as instructed.

"Okay. Take us to the office." A blink, and we appeared in the reception area, startling a shriek out of a pair of women Kate was showing out. "Sorry."

Mr. Whitehaven silently appeared from around the corner, while Kate smiled and told the women, "Nothing to worry about. I'll be in touch."

As they left, I crawled onto the sofa and closed my eyes. "We found something."

"That gave you a headache. Right. I'll get the ibuprofen."

"I love you so much right now."

"What did you find, Discordia?"

Danielle answered Whitehaven before I could. "A disguised portal to the demon realm. Possibly a trap."

"Where?"

She gave him not only the general address, but the exact location down to feet past the buildings' corners and that it was on the east side of the alley.

Damn, she was good.

"Here we go. Sit up, Jones."

I opened my eyes and obeyed, taking a paper cup of water and the pills from Kate. "We need to shut it before someone else falls in."

"I'll call David," Mr. Whitehaven said. "He can handle the matter. Do you need the rest of the day off?"

"No, I'll be fine in a little bit." I needed to take Danielle home. "Oh crap. Need to call Dane. He's still out there."

Yanking out my phone, I dialed quickly.

"Hey, where are you? I'm back in the..." he said, before the line went dead.

I face-palmed. "Leglin, will you please go check if Dane just fell into that place? And bring him here if he did?"

"*Of course.*" My hound disappeared and reappeared a breath later, with Dane holding onto his collar.

"Fastest rescue this side of the Pecos," my partner said, letting go to ruffle Leglin's ears. "Thanks."

He looked around, and didn't seem surprised to see Danielle. Guess she did work in that area. "Thinking I don't need to tell you what just happened."

"Nope, we found it first. Would you mind going back to stand guard until David gets there to close it?"

"Don't mind at all, but I'll need a ride."

"I can drive you," Tabitha said, leaving her desk. "If that's all right?"

Mr. Whitehaven nodded. "Yes, it is. You should be armed. I'll be back in a moment."

The boss left the reception area for his office. I looked at my partner. "You need a way home, and I need my car."

I tossed him my keys, and Dane grinned, catching them. "You're letting me drive Baby?"

"No racing, no scratches, or you're grounded for a month, mister."

"Yes, mom. Where do you want to meet?"

I thought about it for a second. "My house."

Mr. Whitehaven returned with his demon killing sword, and handed it to Dane.

"Thanks. See you after a while." He turned to leave, opening the door for Tabitha as she slipped on her coat.

"Dane."

He looked over his shoulder. "Yes?"

"Be careful."

"I will. Bye."

"Bye. I watched him leave, listening while the boss called David. Did finding the portal trap have anything to do with our case or the curse on me? I looked at Kate. "How likely is it that there's only the one portal to the demon realm?"

"Well, it's the second one you've found."

"No clue, huh?"

Kate shook her head. Danielle decided to sit down, choosing a chair across from the couch. Leglin laid his chin on my knee. I petted his head, thinking. "Is it easy for them to open these portals? Are they the same as entrances to the Barrows or sidhes?"

Mr. Whitehaven ended his call. "It takes a fair amount of power to open portals. The longer they exist, the stronger they become."

"Okay, we don't want any staying open then, because they could become permanent. Right?"

"Correct. The best defense is to close them as soon as they're discovered."

I frowned. "It wasn't there the first time, and I know we walked over that spot earlier today. Why was it open now?"

"Why didn't it smell like demons down there to me?" Danielle asked, wrinkling her nose. "They have a distinctive odor."

"Neither Logan nor Nick could smell demons when they were wearing human bodies." I felt my frown becoming a scowl. "So if you didn't smell demon stink, that could mean they're trapping humans to possess them, or only possessed humans come and go through that portal."

Kate sighed. "I'll talk to Damian, see if there's any missing persons reports that involve that area."

"Thanks." Now what? We had no new leads on our case. I wasn't going to go wandering around the demon realm until we had an idea of what they were up to. "Hm."

Danielle was watching me. "What?"

"I'm trying to figure out whether demons have anything to do with our case."

"You don't know?"

I shook my head. "I mean, I think it's our case, because the first time I got a trail, it was after touching the dust cloth the missing mirror was covered with. But that could be coincidence, because my abilities don't exactly behave logically most of the time. But we have footage of the mirror's theft, and the thief wasn't human."

After I closed my mouth, I blinked. "Wait a minute. Demons can manipulate shadows."

"Demon lords can," Mr. Whitehaven corrected me. "The average demon cannot."

"Great. I guess the demons are case-related then." I wasn't looking forward to tangling with them again. The first time had been scary enough. "If they have the mirror, it could be anywhere."

Danielle suddenly laughed.

"What's so funny?"

"I understand why our Queen is insistent that we guard you. You're a magnet for trouble."

"Gee, thanks."

She shook her head. "That wasn't intended as an insult. I was thinking about what you said earlier."

"Oh." She meant the pawn thing. "Yeah, I get it."

The boss broke in. "If the mirror's in the demon realm, it may not be recoverable."

I looked at him. "Is that you're way of telling me not to go poking around down there?"

"Yes."

"Strangely, I don't feel the need to argue, unless my abilities throw something out."

He nodded. "Of course, but don't go alone. Dane may keep the sword for now, and I'll fetch the dagger for you."

"Thanks, boss." When he left the reception area again, I patted Leglin's head before looking at Danielle. "Guess when he gets back, I'll teleport you home, and go home myself."

She agreed, and that's what I did, once the boss handed over the dagger.

SEVENTEEN

I was outside with the dogs when Dane brought my car home. Once he exited and returned my keys, I asked, "How'd it go?"

"No trouble at all. Didn't see anything or catch a whiff of demon." My partner covered a yawn. "Pretty boring, until Jo and Trixie arrived. Closing a portal makes a lot of glowing special effects. That part was cool."

"David didn't do it?"

Dane shook his head. "Jo said he's cranky today. Some shipment didn't arrive when it was supposed to."

"Oh." David could be fussy about lateness. "Want something to drink?"

"Sure."

"Go on in." The dogs were heading toward the house, finished with their business. "I'll be in with the dogs in a minute."

"Okay." Dane went inside, and I followed once the dogs had all reached the porch.

"Juice, tea, or coffee?" I walked to the kitchen. My partner was seated at the breakfast bar.

"Juice is fine. This case isn't moving fast."

"Some don't. One of my first cases took nearly four months to solve." I collected a couple of glasses. "Ice?"

"Please. I hope this one doesn't take that long. I doubt our client's the patient type."

Selecting orange juice from the options in the fridge, I filled the glasses three-quarters full before dropping ice cubes into each. "Yeah, probably not. But it's kind of hard to figure out supernatural crimes when it comes to shadow magic."

Actually, most magic. It was why I'd preferred vampire cases. They were predators, driven by hunger and power. Pretty simple stuff, or so I'd thought for quite a while.

Then I'd met Derrick and his dhampyr son, Stone. I'd gotten a glimpse into vampire family life from the murders of Lady Esme and her family.

"Right, and elves never have clear reasons for anything."

"Tell me about it." I turned away to put the juice back in the fridge, and turned back—straight into a vision. "Ooh, maybe we have a clue happening."

"What?"

"Vision." I held out my hand and heard Dane leave his stool. "It's a tunnel, rock."

"What color of rock?"

"Reddish."

"It's really freaky when you have visions. Your face goes blank." Dane had reached me, and took my hand. "And your eyes... whoa."

"Whoa, wha... holy crap, dude." I stared at him in the tunnel's dim light. "How the hell did you get in here?"

My partner blinked, his nostrils flaring and eyes opening wide. "I don't know. Wow, this feels real. Smells real, too. Are all your visions like this?"

"No, just the retrocogs. Oh, and the precogs, I guess."

He looked both ways down the tunnel. "Not gonna lie, this is kind of cool. What do we do?"

"I usually wait for something to happen, but this looks like the same kind of tunnel we found earlier." Which meant demons, and I'd had the terrifying experience of having a demon see me in a vision before.

Dane apparently felt my shiver at that memory, because his grip tightened. "How about we not do the usual?"

"Sounds good. Which way?" Should I call Leglin over? The hound had entered a vision before. Yet, realistic as my visions could be, Leglin couldn't transport me out of one.

"Left? The tunnel slopes down that direction."

It did? "Why down?"

Dane grinned. "If this is the demon realm, the deeper we go, the more chance we have of seeing them. If we see them..."

"We'll catch some clues. Okay." I didn't really want to go deeper into the demon realm, but not being stuck in a vision alone was nice. "Don't let go."

"I won't. Ready?"

"Yeah."

We began walking. Nervousness opened my mouth. "Where is the light coming from?"

"It's some kind of fungus, mixed in the rock."

"Doesn't it need sunlight to recharge?"

"Nope."

So much for that outlet. "Demons are *Numero Dos* on my Bad Guy List."

Dane glanced my way. "Who's Number One?"

"Gods."

"Number Three?"

"Elves."

"Our lists match," he said. "There's a three-way intersection ahead. I've been meaning to ask you something."

"What?"

"Why can't you transform stuff?"

"Huh?"

"You kind of do, I mean. You do that thing with air, making it thicker. That's transformational."

Grateful for a distracting subject, I shrugged. "I don't think that's the same thing as what you guys can do."

"Maybe not exactly, but isn't teleportation a transformation? You move from one place to another, and you're not exactly anywhere for a second or two. Right?"

"Yeah, but I don't know that it's an actual transformation. Right or left?" We'd reached the intersection. I couldn't tell if either part of the new tunnel sloped up or down.

"Right."

"It slopes down?"

"No, but there's some doors set in the walls. I think we should check them out."

"Sure."

"You transform air to fire or ice."

I nodded. "Yeah, but that's about friction. Make air move faster, or rather its molecules, and it gets hot. Slow the molecules down, and the water vapor solidifies."

"That only makes me wonder more, since you can change air at the molecular level." Dane peered through a barred opening in the first door we'd reached. "Empty."

I looked too. "It's a cell."

"Yep. Let's keep going."

We backed away and walked to the next door. My partner continued the conversation. "I mean, if you can make air molecules do what you want, why shouldn't you be able to make other molecules do what you want?"

The next cell was also empty. "Give me a for instance."

"Well, what about changing your shape?"

I pulled him to a halt. "What?"

"Why couldn't you learn how to do that?" Dane shrugged. "You've been in a different shape before."

"Because of a cursing potion."

"Well, yeah, but seriously. You can do stuff."

I cocked my head, studying his expression. "Do you know something I don't about my abilities?"

"Maybe? I started poking around, after we returned from the Unseelie realm. The Unseelie and Kethyrdryll said you were a natural mage. We should probably keep moving."

"Yeah." I let him pull me along. "Why would their label make you poke around?"

"This one's empty, too. Because Kethyrdryll said you were descended from all the great families, and that they started because the gods were having affairs with humans."

"Empty," I said, checking the fourth cell. "And?"

"Gods can transform themselves and others into anything, Cordi."

"But I'm not a god."

"No, but legends say their half-human children—natural mages—could transform themselves or others, too. Empty. We have one door left before a turn to the right."

"So you think I should be able to change shape."

"Makes sense."

We paused to look into the last cell. "Holy crap. It's the mirror."

The mirror's darkened surface glowed green and a misshapen face appeared. "Who's there?"

"Uh-oh." We ducked, looking at each other. I whispered, "Now what?"

"You're the vision expert."

"I can hear you," the mirror said. "And one of you is a woman. Hopefully naked. I requested a TV with the X-rated channels, but the real thing's far better."

"Ugh." Tanisha was correct: The mirror was a pervert. I straightened to look into the cell. "Hello. You can see us?"

"You're right outside my door. Of course I can see you." A leer transformed the mirror's pale green face. "Love to see more. Why don't you come in and..." his leer disappeared. "Oh. I see. You're not really here. Tease."

"Excuse me?"

"Shame. Dark-haired beauties are my favorites."

I frowned. "How do you know we're not really here?"

"I see, hear, and know all," the mirror intoned, his voice deeper than before. "You're a natural mage, peeking into the past. Naughty girl. I like naughty girls."

Rolling my eyes, I said, "We're private investigators, hired to recover you."

"By whom?"

"Celadine." Dane tried the door with his free hand. "Wait, we can't actually do anything in a vision, right?"

"Leglin carried a pebble out of one for me."

"Okay, then maybe if we can open the door, I can carry the mirror out?"

"Ooh, escape from this dreary cell? I like it." The mirror brightened.

"Let me try to pick the lock."

Dane looked away. "Uh, I hear someone coming. If he can see us..."

"They might be able to, too, if they're demons." Crap. So close, even considering our plan might not work.

"So we'd better, hey." Dane scowled as our surroundings changed. We were in my kitchen. "Damn it."

I heaved a sigh, releasing his hand. "It's okay. Now we know exactly where the mirror is."

"What are we going to do?"

"Duh. We're going to steal it back."

EIGHTEEN

"This will totally work. Leglin can take us in and out. All we have to do is grab hold of the mirror. Easy peasy."

Dane scrunched his face. "It could be booby-trapped. Warded."

"Then we'll take Ronnie with us." She was the coven's warding expert. "Do reconnaissance first and let her check it out."

My goal was to do it as quickly and safely as possible. Especially if we were going to involve Ronnie, since she had kids. I knew she'd go, because she'd been part of the cavalry the first time demons had caused trouble. That fight had been a close call, and I did not want to be the reason Ronnie didn't make it home to her hubby and children.

"Maybe we should call the client first," Dane said.

"Yeah, because a clue why demons want the mirror would be nice." I pulled out my cell phone. After connecting, I had to wait for Lady Celadine to come to the phone, because her secretary answered.

Celadine's greeting was a frosty "I do hope you've progress to report, Miss Jones."

Dane grinned when I rolled my eyes. "We've found your mirror, but retrieving it will take a bit longer. Any idea why demons would want it?"

She sucked in a breath. "You will retrieve it immediately. This instant, do you understand?"

"Whoa there, Nelly. We have to plan, because..."

"Now!" She ended the call with that shrieked word. Dane and I winced in reaction.

"Well, it appears it's super important we recover the mirror," he said. "This instant, even."

"That was the impression I got too. Let me call Ronnie."

She answered after a single ring. "Hi, Cordi."

"Hey. Are you busy? We kind of need your expertise on a case."

Ronnie hissed. "Oops, sorry. That was cold. Uh, I'm kind of in the middle of a doctor appointment."

"Are you okay?"

She laughed, and I heard a weird sound from her end. "I'm great. We're looking at our next baby right now."

"Oh, wow. Congratulations."

"Thank you. Number four." She paused when someone spoke too low for me to hear. "I'll be done here in about twenty or thirty minutes. Where do you want to meet?"

Dane began shaking his head, mirroring my feelings, so I said, "Well, here's the thing. We've been hired to retrieve a stolen mirror, and found it, in the demon realm. So maybe you can suggest someone else?"

"Oh, yeah. I don't want to go there right now. Um, let's see," she was silent for a moment. "If you can pry him out of the shop, David would be best. If not him, Jo would be my next choice. They're both pretty good with wards, but they'll need a little more time than I do."

"All right, thanks. Congratulations again." We traded "Byes" and I ended the call. "I'll try David first."

"Let's just go over there. It'll cut down on time."

I eyed him. "Do you have a date?"

"At seven."

"Ooh, are things getting serious?" I pushed away from my desk to stand up.

"My answer depends on whether you're going to tease me."

Grabbing my purse and jacket, I laughed. "You mean the way you tease me about Logan?"

"Yeah."

"I'm going to tease the holy crap out of you."

Dane laughed. "Meanie. Okay, yeah, maybe serious. Not 'settle down forever' serious, but possibly 'this could lead to long-term dating' serious."

I didn't give him a hard time. "That's great."

"I think so too." He took the hand I held out, and I teleported us to the Blue Orb.

Jo waved to us from her spot behind the tall counter. "Hey, guys."

"Hey. Is David around?"

"He's with a customer. What's up?" She folded her arms and leaned on the counter. I explained why we were there, leaving out the call to Ronnie, and Jo wrinkled her nose. "Why haven't you called Ronnie?"

"We did, but she just found out she's pregnant," Dane said. Jo squealed, but I shot him a dirty look. "What?"

"You don't tell people that kind of thing without permission. It's Ronnie's news to share."

"Oh, sorry. I didn't know that was a rule."

"Don't tell anyone else."

He pretended to zip his lips. "I won't, promise."

"Argh." Jo mock-scowled. "Now I have to sit on the news too."

I pointed at Dane, swinging my finger to Jo. "See the turmoil you've caused? Do you?"

He dropped to both knees, holding up his clasped hands. "Please, oh please, forgive me for this terrible social faux paus."

We were laughing when Tonya came out of the back room. "What's funny?"

"Dane. He's being a dork." I looked at Jo while my partner climbed to his feet. "So what are the chances of taking David away from all of this for a little while?"

"Higher than usual, thanks to a gaggle of sorority girl wannabe witches." She and Tonya rolled their eyes in perfect unison. "They were shopping for love potion ingredients."

"Do those work?" Not that I'd ever use one. Just curious.

The two witches snorted in tandem, and I fought a smile. Jo answered. "No, love potions don't work. Especially not the one they were talking about. But there are potions and spells that can give the magic user control over his or her victim's emotions. Those usually take someone with major talent. Spells are all about intent. The form and ingredients are just tools to focus that intent."

I squinted at her. "Thorandryll took an awful long time mixing up that potion to change me back."

Jo shrugged. "He was having to guess what Dalsarin's true intent was for cursing you, and counteract it. Magic's actually sort of complicated most of the time."

"Anyway, it's a good thing love spells don't work," Tonya said. "What does work can be messy enough. Like, violently messy."

"Why would anyone want something that wasn't real?" Dane leaned on the counter.

"Well, that's kind of the problem with people wanting to do love spells. Hearsay is that love potions only work if the victim already has romantic feelings for the person. Basically, people think a potion just speeds things up." Tonya grinned when Jo patted her on the head. "I'm a good student witch."

"They're party poopers anyway. Half the fun's in getting there."

I agreed with Dane's statement with a nod of my head, having well-learned the lesson of rushing ahead in relationships.

We moved down the counter when David appeared with a customer in tow. He wasn't wearing his customary cardigan, and the sleeves of his pale blue Oxford shirt were rolled up. No glasses perched at the tip of his nose, or sat askew on top of his head. He was in pure business mode, something I'd rarely seen. Giving the customer her receipt, bag, and a broad, plastic-looking smile, David said, "Thank you, and please do come again."

Once the customer left, the bell over the door tinkling, he looked at Dane and me. "I didn't hear you come in."

"Teleported. Came to see if you're in the mood for a field trip."

David's face brightened. "Where?"

"Demon realm."

"I'm in," he said before I'd finished speaking. "Let me grab a few things."

He hurried off to the back room, and Jo giggled. "Told you. Try and keep him in one piece, okay?"

I saluted her. "Aye, Captain, we'll do our best."

David returned, slinging a dark brown, leather messenger bag onto the counter. "Almost ready."

We watched him trot upstairs. I looked at Jo. "He didn't even ask what we needed him to do."

She laughed. "I don't think he cares. Tell him when you get there."

"What if he needs something he doesn't have in here?" I poked at the messenger bag.

"Me." The voice was a croak, and I raised my head to find Copernicus, David's raven familiar, perched on top of the shelves to our left. He stretched his wings before gliding down and landing on the bag.

"Ask a dumb question." I ran my hand over the bird's back. "Hello."

"Cordi." Copernicus inclined his head. He'd never spoken to me before I'd been turned into a dog. Percy, Kate's parrot, talked all the time. I wondered if Trixie, Illy, or Saki, the other familiars, could talk. They all understood people just fine, based on past experience.

Once upon a time, I'd wished for a familiar of my own, thinking such a companion would help keep me from freaking out when scared. Now, I had someone comparable. "I'd better call my hound. Leglin."

The huge, black and tan hound silently appeared. Elf hounds looked like a cross between an Irish wolfhound and a Rottweiler, just larger. I turned to pat him, and he hit Dane with his wagging tail. "Hey, buddy. We need your help."

"I am always pleased to be of assistance."

Dane limped a few feet, rubbing his thigh. "Remind me to step back when you call him, because ow."

"Sorry." I fought a grin.

"Ready!" David sang, thumping down the stairs. He'd changed into brown cargo pants, a white camp shirt, hiking boots, and to top it all off, a brown leather bomber's jacket.

Tonya took off for another part of the store, trailing muffled giggles in her wake as David plopped the brown fedora he carried onto his head. Jo gave me a long-suffering, "See what I have to put up with?" look. "You forgot the whip."

"Don't tease him. He's David, Man of Action."

"Hah," said the newly dubbed Man of Action. "Cordi doesn't think I'm weird."

"Oh, I do, but it's a weirdness I can totally get behind." I tried to mimic a movie voice-over tone. "Mild-mannered shopkeeper by day, daring adventurer by night."

David beamed. "I'm cool."

"You're awesome."

Jo groaned. "Stop encouraging him. He's been drooling over a Thor costume."

"For next Halloween." David offered his arm to his raven. Copernicus side-walked up to his shoulder and squatted, avoiding the fedora's brim. Next, he pulled the bag's strap over the bird and his head, settling it on the opposite shoulder. "Let's go."

"Okay. Leglin, we need you to take us to the demon realm."

My hound immediately dropped his big rear end to the floor, his ears flattening. "*It's a dangerous place.*"

"I know, but the thing we need to close a case is there. I can show you exactly where it is."

Leglin cocked his head, but didn't relax his ears. "*Will we have to stay there long?*"

"That depends on David. But Copernicus is going." I hooked my forefingers behind his ears to unflatten them. "None of us wants to be there any longer than necessary."

Leglin heaved a sigh and stood. "*Very well.*"

While the men took places on either side of him, I summoned my memory of the room the mirror was in, and carefully transferred that image to the hound via telepathy. "Can you see it?"

Leglin flicked one ear. "*Is this how humans see?*"

Crap, would it not work? I didn't remember anything looking super different as a dog. Except red had appeared yellow. "Yeah. Can you take us there?"

"*How did it smell?*"

Argh. "Sorry, I don't have a dog nose anymore."

"He wants the scent?"

"Yeah."

Dane nodded. "Can you do whatever you're doing with my memory of it? It might be closer to what's normal for him."

"Okay, but you have to concentrate on just that memory. Like, really hard. I don't want to trip into any personal stuff."

"Right. Okay." Dane closed his eyes. "I've got it. Now what?"

"I'm going to look into your mind. You shouldn't feel anything." I focused carefully, and linked to him telepathically. "Here we go."

"*Much better,*" Leglin said. "*I know where to take you now.*"

"Awesome." I broke the links to both of their minds. "Then we're ready to go. Everyone touch Leglin."

They obeyed, and a second later, we were in the tunnel from my vision.

<hr />

David scowled, an unusual expression for him. "Who touched the door?"

"I did."

"Advice for the future: Don't touch doors in the demon realm unless you want them to know you're here."

Dane ducked his head, his ears reddening. "It's warded?"

"Yes. How can you assume the mirror's warded, but not think the door it's behind is?"

I broke in. David could lecture at Mom level when the mood struck him. "It was a vision. We didn't know we could set off wards in a vision."

"Now you do." David looked into the cell. "Hm. We need to get inside without opening the door. The ward on it has been reset."

"Okay." I patted Leglin. "Take a look, then take us in."

My hound rose on his hind legs, planting one paw on Dane's shoulder. After a second or two, he dropped back to all fours. "*Ready.*"

We all made contact with him, and were instantly inside the cell. The mirror's surface stayed dark.

"Listen for trouble," David said, crossing to the mirror. "We'll need a few minutes."

"Sure." Dane, Leglin, and I stayed near the door. I strained my ears watching what was viewable of the tunnel outside, and heard a whole lot of nothing.

The soft rustle of Copernicus' wings turned my head. The raven was on the floor, his head cocked. He began to walk around the mirror. A glance at David showed me his slack face and unfocused eyes.

I looked at the raven again, considering whether this picture was alright.

Copernicus disappeared behind the mirror, reappearing on its other side two breaths later.

David moved, startling me. "Right, then. It is warded. We can remove the ward, but it'll take about fifteen minutes."

"Okay. Do what you gotta do."

"We will, but you'll need to be quiet so we can concentrate. Nothing louder than breathing, please."

"We'll be quiet unless we have to sound the alarm," Dane said.

A greenish glow filled the room, and the mirror spoke. "You're back, and you brought a warlock. Delightful."

"Great. Look, we're going to get you out, but you need to be quiet so the warlock can take care of the ward on you."

"I'll be quiet if you take your clothes off."

Gah. "I'm not doing that. Don't you want to go home?"

"Would everyone please shut up so we can start? Unwinding a ward like this requires careful precision." David glared first at the mirror, then at me. The mirror made a rude suggestion that heated my face, even though it wasn't directed at me.

David was unfazed. "Charming. Now shut up before my familiar steps in."

The elongated, pale face tilted down to study the raven. "Steve, is that you?"

"Quiet." Copernicus' croak of an order accomplished what neither David nor I had been able to. The mirror sniffed and its surface went dark.

David echoed the sniff, checking the set of his fedora. "Finally."

I traded a smile with Dane before returning to watching the tunnel. Light flashed behind us in multi-colored hues.

Unable to stop myself, I looked and discovered David had picked up Thorandryll's trick of inscribing symbols in the air. His right hand stabbed and swooped while his familiar's head bobbed to some internal tune.

It was pretty cool to watch. David created layer after layer of glowing symbols, moving counter-clockwise around the mirror.

Several minutes later, he halted in front of the mirror and snapped his fingers. The covering of symbols blazed and shattered.

"Someone's coming," Dane said. "And fast."

I blinked. David and Copernicus were gone. "Crap. Did he do it?"

"Don't know. We gotta go." My partner grabbed my arm and Leglin's collar. "The shop, please."

"But," I closed my mouth, the shop around us instead of the cell. "Damn it."

"Where's the mirror?" David asked, unslinging his bag.

"How did you get back here?"

"Me." Copernicus launched from David's shoulder.

"We didn't know if you were done." Dane released my arm.

"Yes."

"Great." I huffed and crossed my arms. "We have to go back, and they'll probably reset the ward."

"No, they won't." David twirled his fedora on his finger. "They won't realize it's gone. I wove an illusion clone."

"A what?"

Jo smirked, patting David's leather-clad shoulder. "He made it look as though it's still warded, but it isn't."

"Oh. Awesome. Okay, let's go back."

Dane shook his head. "How about we wait for a little while, and let whoever was coming clear off?"

"Because they might move it."

"Maybe. If they do, we'll search for it."

"Argh." I glared at him.

"Better safe than sorry."

"Oh, alright. Let's go to the office and update the boss." I let my arms drop to my sides. "Thanks, David. You're the bomb."

He took a bow. "You're welcome."

NINETEEN

"We found the mirror."

Mr. Whitehaven smiled. "Excellent. Where is it?"

"Demon realm. Don't worry. We took David and Copernicus with us. The mirror was warded, but David took care of that." I dropped into a chair. "We had a tiny miscommunication issue, because Copernicus whisked David out before we were certain he'd finished."

"Someone was coming. We left," Dane clarified. "Giving it a few minutes before going back to grab the mirror."

"I see."

"I think just Leglin and I should go. We'll blink right back if someone's there, or the mirror's been moved." I frowned. "Where's the dust cloth? I want to cover him. The mirror."

"I'll get it." Dane left the boss's office.

"Any new cases in line?" I kept talking to keep Mr. Whitehaven from protesting the plan we'd made.

"Nothing yet."

"Cool."

Dane returned, tossing the sheet to me. "Here you go."

"Thanks. Think it's been long enough?"

"Probably."

"Good." I stood, sheet in one hand. "Come on, Leglin. Let's steal ourselves a mirror."

My hound shoved his head under my other hand, and my fingers slid down to his collar. "We'll be back in a minute, in the reception area."

"Be careful."

"We will. Okay, Leglin." No more office. We were in the cell and alone. The mirror stood in its spot. "Great. Just a sec."

I shook out the dust cloth and covered the mirror, with Leglin staying close. Done, I grabbed hold of the mirror and the hound. "Take us out, bub."

My hound took us back to the office, and I let go of both, smiling at those waiting for us. "Easy, peasy."

"I'll inform the client," Mr. Whitehaven said. "Excellent work."

He left for his office. Dane walked over. "Let's take off the cloth."

"So Creepy McCreeperson can talk crap to Tabitha and me? No, thanks." I'd had my fill of Mr. Mouthbreather Spirit Jerk. "But if Kate comes in, I bet twenty she'll shut him down in less than a minute."

"I'm not taking that bet." He grinned. "And I think you're overestimating. I give her ten seconds."

"I was adding in time for her to make Percy be quiet. He would think Creepy is a hoot." I hadn't forgotten the parrot's X-rated suggestions the one time he'd visited the New Age center where my mom worked.

Recalling that event, I wondered what elves would think of humans' attempts to infuse crystals with positive vibes. Which reminded me that I had a large, embarrassingly shaped crystal hidden in a shoebox in my closet.

That had been loads of fun, retrieving the crystal after Logan had found it under the seat of my car. He'd barely begun working on the car, and hello! How about a big honking, pink phallic crystal in your face, Mr. Sayer?

As though conjured by the memory, Logan's dark green, classic Challenger slowed to pull into the parking lot. Heat warmed my face, which was silly, because no one knew what I'd just been thinking. "Hey, Logan's here."

"And your face is pink," Dane said. "Coincidence? I think not."

"Shut up."

He laughed. "Blushing is usually the result of embarrassment. Why would Logan showing up embarrass you? Unless you two have done more than snuggle lately."

"Nope, we haven't, Nosey Man. Hush." Logan was on his way to the door. "I was thinking about something else, not him."

"Sure you were."

"Grrr."

Logan opened the door and came inside. He glanced at the covered mirror while saying hello. "You retrieved it."

"Yep. The boss is calling the client to come get it."

"Any problems?"

I laughed. "Leglin and I make an awesome cat-burgling team. We were in and out in less than three seconds, no demons the wiser."

"We're all grateful you use your powers for good."

"And hope you don't have an evil twin," Dane added.

"I'm a one-of-a-kind model. My mom says so." I looked at Logan. "Are you here to talk to the boss? He's in his office."

"I am. Talk to you after?"

I nodded and he left the reception area. Dane stopped poking at the dust cloth. "I guess I'll go finish the report. Case closed."

"Okay." I plopped down onto the couch and smiled at Tabitha. "So, has Damian asked you out yet?"

She folded her arms on the desk's edge. "He has."

"And you said?"

"Yes."

"Awesome. He's a good guy."

Tabitha smiled. "I think so, too."

I patted Leglin, who'd sat close enough to lay his head across my knees. "What are you going to do? Dinner and a movie, or something else?"

"Dinner and bowling."

"Bowling," I repeated. "My parents used to take me when I was a kid. We always had fun."

"I've never done it, so he'll have to teach me."

"I'm sure he won't mind."

Tabitha glanced down the hallway before asking, "Is it difficult to learn?"

"Not really. Takes some practice to learn how to keep score and play, but the main point of it is to use a ball to knock down pins." Maybe Logan and I could go bowling this weekend. I made a mental note to ask him.

We chit-chatted a bit longer, before Logan returned. "Sorry to interrupt."

"No problem. Well?"

He grinned. "I start tomorrow."

"Yay." I jumped to my feet to hug him. "This calls for a celebration. Dinner, my treat?"

"Sounds good."

We bade Tabitha goodbye, and walked out to Logan's car, Leglin trailing behind us. "I'd better send him home."

"I don't mind, if he doesn't. He'll fit in the back seat."

"Up to you, Leglin."

"I will go home. Please thank him for the offer."

"Sure. He said thanks, but he's going home." I waved my hand right after Leglin disappeared. "And ta-dah!"

Chuckling, Logan opened the passenger door. "Where do you want to go?"

"Your choice."

He chose Chinese, buffet style. We filled our plates with fried rice, black pepper chicken for me, and General Tsao's for him.

Once we were seated at our table, Logan asked, "Any headway on your curse problem?"

"Haven't had time to concentrate on it, but I plan to work on it tonight." I crunched a fried wonton. "Have you ever bowled?"

"Bo... oh. No, can't say I have. Why?"

"Thought we could do that this weekend. I haven't been to a bowling alley in ages."

Logan smiled. "I'm game."

"Cool."

TWENTY

One of the best things about working for Arcane Solutions was not having to punch a clock on a daily basis.

Mr. Whitehaven wanted to retain his employees, so he paid us a comfortable base salary, which meant we didn't have to look for second jobs to make ends meet when business was slow.

It also meant we were always on call, and we seldom had any lengthy slow periods. The past six months had been busy enough that I was glad he'd hired Dane, and now Logan.

More cases equaled more money for everyone. Since we all got along well, and had no cooperation issues, no one ever got stuck working a case alone, if they needed help.

All of which meant, with no new cases currently in the pipeline, I was free to concentrate on my personal case.

Once home, I sat and made a list of suspects who had grudges against me. Apep, Eater of Souls, made the top of the chart. Hesitation struck as I began to write "vampires," because while I knew there were a few who probably wanted some revenge, the vampire Council currently liked me. At least enough to not want me permanently dead for now. "Better add them anyway. Dark elves, if Dalsarin wasn't really the last one?"

Yep. I wrote that down. "Demons?"

Screwing up their plans had put me on their naughty list, even if they didn't yet know about Strike Two: stealing the mirror back.

"Who else?" I thought it over and sighed. "Nick?"

My delusions had begun not long after I'd broken things off with him. Of course, they had started after the fight with Merriven, too.

Nick had said he loved me, and was serious enough to buy a ring. Love could cause people to do crazy things.

So could rejection.

Diablo wandered in, and came to stand beside my chair.

"Am I looking at this the right way?"

"*Looking at what?*" Diablo reared to plant his paws on the desk's edge, and sniffed at the paper. "*Is there more than one way to look at paper?*"

I scratched the back of his neck. "Not the paper, the situation."

"*Case?*"

"Curse."

The black pit perked his ears. "*You're not a dog again.*"

"No this curse makes me see things that aren't there."

"*Oh. So that's what your problem is.*" Diablo flicked an ear and leaned into my scratching. "*You been acting like a Mexican jumping bean.*"

"Sorry." I turned and began using both hands to scratch him. His black hair was short, but thick and shiny.

"*You haven't been jumping lately.*"

"Someone removed the curse from me, but I have to find out who cursed me."

Diablo dropped to the floor. "*My money's on Smelly.*"

"Smelly?"

"*That wolf you were cozy with. Wolves are bad news.*"

"Why would he curse me?"

"*Because you kicked 'im to the curb instead of being his mate.*" Diablo's face wrinkled. "*Want us to get him?*"

"No, but thanks for the offer." I patted his head and swiveled my chair back to the desk. After giving the dog's opinion some serious consideration, I picked up the pen, and added Nick's name to the list. Not that I really thought he'd go that far, but it also wasn't as though I'd known him for years.

Diablo grunted before wandering out of my office.

Shifters were basically magic people, based on what I'd learned about their origins. But could they create actual spells?

Of course, David's shop stayed in business on the principle that anyone could create magic by using the right spells and ingredients. If only certain people could, the Blue Orb wouldn't be nearly as successful as it was.

Staring at Nick's name, I mentally face-palmed. I had an expert I could ask, right next door: Moira.

As the clan's shamaness, she'd know what shifters could do when it came to using magic. I could also talk to her about seeing the ancestors, and my worries over the missing White Queen.

A call to Logan assured me that the dogs were always welcome in clan territory, and netted an offer to guide me to Moira's house.

He met us just past the parking lot, greeting me with a hug. I returned it with interest, wondering how much longer I'd be able to hold out before diving into bed with him.

"I let her know you were on the way over, and I'll keep an eye on Speck and Squishy," he said as we disengaged. Re-engagement followed instantly, his hand sliding around mine. "If you need me to."

"Thanks." We walked down the path, our pace slow due to the dogs' need to sniff everything. I didn't mind, because it meant longer hand-holding time. The air was cool and pine-scented, but I felt warmer than I had on my walk over. "Is the whole territory like this?"

"No, there's rainforest, grasslands, even a mangrove swamp, and highlands. We needed a mix of habitats, since we have a mix of tiger breeds. Most clans do."

"Cool." I was not going to waste brain power on how they'd done that. Maybe someday a headache wouldn't be the result of trying to comprehend magic, but today wasn't that day. "If there's a beach around, I'll take my next vacation here."

Logan stepped over Squishy, who'd found something interesting to sniff on the path. "We don't have ocean access, but there's lakes and rivers. One goes through the jungle area, and it has a few nice beach spots."

"What about snakes and piranhas? Or alligators?"

"None of those. We're the apex predators here, though we have some small predators to keep things in balance." He squeezed my fingers. "There's a troupe of chimpanzees in the rainforest, and Michelle—she's one of our Bengals—saw a few groups of smaller monkeys. We have some foxes and buzzards too."

"That's too cool."

"Even cooler: They're sort of programmed to let us know when something's wrong." He half-smiled. "They're real wild animals, but not. It's kind of hard to explain, but the reasoning is that we'll be able to help them if there's injuries or illnesses, because they'll come to us."

"Kind of a fail-safe, huh? To keep all this on an even keel?"

He nodded. "Exactly. They won't avoid us completely, so we'll see them, but it's better to keep our distance unless necessary."

"What about deer or rabbits? Will they come to tell you if something's wrong?"

"No, since they're our main prey animals. It's up to us to be good shepherds, weed out the sick or injured, and not over hunt the healthy."

I wrinkled my nose, but didn't protest. Animals hunted other animals. That's how the circle of life worked in the wild. "I think I'll skip the hunts."

Logan chuckled in response. We'd reached the main street and its houses, but he led me down it, past the big community building. Also past the playground and the gathering area where we'd celebrated Solstice. "Moira wanted space. It's easier for people to seek her out when they need her help, if she's not smack in the middle of everything."

Her house was a really cute log cabin, set in the trees not far from the edge of the gathering ground. The cabin wasn't particularly large, but it had a covered front porch big enough to hang out on. We didn't go to the front door, but around back. I stopped, impressed by the space behind the cabin. There was a clearing, but the trees edging it weren't pines, and their branches met overhead to form a canopy. "Neat. It's like a natural gazebo."

Moira waved at us. She was sitting in one of the Adirondack style wooden chairs arranged around an in-ground fire pit at the center of the area. Her welcoming smile reinforced the friendliness I'd noticed in her from the start. "Come have a seat."

The three big dogs agreed to a run with Logan, while my two Chihuahuas thought warm laps were a better idea.

In short order, I was sitting by the fire pit close to Moira, each of us with a lump of snoozing fur in our laps.

That was when I felt a little unnerved, because I knew she and Logan were exes. It made it difficult for me to think of how to start the conversation.

Moira waited for a couple minutes before taking pity on me. "Logan said you needed help with something?"

"Yes. Did he tell you I was cursed? I mean, again?"

"He did, and that a gargoyle gave you a Tear to block it."

"Yeah." I petted Squishy. Speck was in Moira's lap. "Lord Kadon removed the curse, but I'm trying to figure out who cursed me."

"Okay." She gave a slight nod.

"My suspect list is limited, and there's a name on it I kind of hate having there. Nick's."

"Ah." Moira pursed her lips. "We, meaning shifters in general, aren't magically powerful. Our magic is shifting shape." Her lips curved. "Plus the physical benefits. Speed, strength, and quick healing."

"So Nick can't be the one who did it."

Moira slowly shook her head. "He can't create and throw a curse, no, but he could hire the job out. The question is: Do you really think he'd want to harm you?"

I answered without thinking. "No. Okay, scratching him off the list. That leaves..."

Her eyebrows rose when I trailed off. "Yes?"

Something was dancing right at the edge of my mind. "I've been cursed three times."

"Some girls have all the luck," Moira murmured.

"Yeah, right. Okay, the first time it was passed by touch." The dark elf, Dalsarin, had gone on a cursing spree and sent a gunman to my little brother's school. But it wasn't the gunman who'd passed the curse. It was the police chief. We'd never figured out how Dalsarin had come into contact with him. I felt my forehead wrinkling.

"The second time it was a potion." Also a present from Dalsarin, personally presented.

Moira nodded, watching me intently. I stared back, trying not to wrestle with the teasing memory. "I don't know how I was cursed this time."

"Well, not that I would deal in curses if I could, but I do know something about them." She stroked Speck's round head with her forefinger. "A potion or an object is the usual method. If it's neither of those, then it's a long-distance spell. Those require a focus object."

My surroundings disappeared and I blinked.

"Cordi?"

"Vision." Everything was dark. Where the hell was I? I lifted my hand and felt Moira take hold of it.

"Oh my. It's dark," she whispered. "I can barely see."

Pulling tiger shifters into my visions was becoming a thing. "Is it the clan bond?"

Moira understood my question. "Could be."

"Can you make out anything?"

"Barely. We're in a cavern, I think. There's a wall close. Is it possible to turn around? I feel a lot of open space behind us."

"Yeah, I think so." It was weird, sitting still and trying to turn around, but we sort of shuffled.

The shamaness hissed. "I see you."

"Who?"

"You," she said, right before light blazed.

I blinked and shuddered as Merriven's voice broke the silence. "Once you've learned your place, you'll begin your new existence in truth, as my little princess."

Now I understood what Moira had meant. The vampire stood over my past self. It was a retrocog vision.

I glanced at the tiger, whose eyes were dark orange and unblinking as she stared at the tableau.

"So much wrong with that sentence." Wow, I sounded like crap. Looked like it too.

We both twitched when he threatened to feed my dad to me.

"He was a real winner," Moira said.

"Yeah."

She growled when the vamp straddled me, and stopped when I tossed him with telekinesis. Her growl returned when he used TK to yank me upright and pull me across the cavern to him.

"Yeah, that sucked, and," I winced, watching Merriven sink his teeth into my neck. "That's really disgusting. Why does anyone think it's sexy? It friggin' hurts."

"Biting's fun, in the right circumstances. Those weren't." Moira's lips tightened.

"Petra's about to show up."

The gargoyle did, dropping like a rock behind Merriven. My past self fell to the rocky floor when the gargoyle hooked her claws into Merriven's sides.

He tore free, turning to face her, only to get her huge left paw to his head. About to follow up with her right, Petra checked.

"I think that's when I told her not to kill him, telepathically."

Moira nodded. The gargoyle leaped, wrapping her front legs around the vamp, and they disappeared. Everything went dark, but we heard my whisper to call my hound.

I couldn't see what happened next, but could hear Logan's voice. "Discord?"

"He's checking you," Moira informed me. "Covering your neck wound. He has Leglin's collar... and you're all three gone now."

"Okay." The vision didn't end. I felt a flutter of panic. "Um..."

"Someone's appeared. A woman." Moira hissed. "She's soaking a cloth in your spilled blood."

"Crap." I sucked in a breath. "What does she look..."

The vision changed, and the shamaness pointed. "That's her."

An even earlier version of my past self, wearing a crimson dress and black robe, sat, while a blonde woman trimmed my hair. Demon Mitchell and his big, scaly, green side-kick stood by watching.

"Well, guess I have the answer." We kept watching, the vision not ending until the blonde was alone, and had carefully collected the tufts of hair she'd trimmed.

Moira blinked as our true surroundings reappeared, and released my hand. "A demon."

"Yep."

"She has your blood and hair." The shamaness frowned. "Cordi..."

"I know. I'm in big trouble." I gave her a hopeful look. "Maybe she used it all?"

"I'd love to be comforting, but I doubt it."

"Fantastic." What the hell was I supposed to do now?

"There's only two ways to end this particular threat. Either recover, or destroy, what she has left." Moira was frowning.

"Which means exploring the demon realm, and that's not exactly the safest place."

She looked at me. "I'm not certain you fully realize the danger you're in. That demon has enough of you to create a killing curse."

"Are you," I closed my mouth, remembering that Dalsarin had cursed people into committing suicide. "Never mind. Okay, I have to act fast. Got it. But if she could do that, why hasn't she? Why curse me with delusions?"

Moira shrugged. "I have no idea. As far as I know, demons' sole pursuit is causing chaos."

"Maybe punishment for interfering?"

"Your guess is as good as mine." She drummed her fingers on the arm of her chair. "You'll need help, but care must be taken in choosing who to ask. You don't want anyone who can use blood and hair against you."

"No elves." I nodded. "And sneaky is the way to go. Going in barrels blazing almost didn't turn out so great, last time."

My cell phone went off, eliciting drowsy grumbles from the Chihuahuas. Squishy slapped at my hand when I pulled the phone from my jacket pocket. "Hang on, it's the boss."

Mr. Whitehaven didn't waste time on a greeting. "I'm afraid we have a problem. The spirit is no longer in the mirror."

"Fan-freaking-tastic."

TWENTY-ONE

Lady Celadine had been ranting since we—Logan, Dane, Leglin, and I—had walked through the door. Her cheeks were flushed, and her grass-green eyes were glaring daggers as she catalogued both our failures to retrieve her property in full and my personal flaws.

"Plain, obviously incompetent, and unbelievably dense."

I rolled my eyes. "Any chance you'll be done soon? Because all you're doing is wasting everyone's time."

"You misbegotten, impertinent, ugly little monster. How dare you..." She pointed a finger in my direction and shrieked when Leglin hit her with his front paws. He knocked her back and down onto the sofa.

Petty satisfaction was mine, seeing the muddy paw prints my hound left on her lovely green dress. Leglin didn't growl, but he did stand in front of her, his eyes locked on hers.

"I'm not the one who failed to keep your stupid mirror safe. I didn't let it get stolen." Crossing my arms, I smiled at her. "Evidently being smart and pretty also means lacking common sense in your case."

"You will not speak to me in such a disrespectful," Celadine tried to push Leglin away. He didn't budge. "Fashion."

"You could've avoided this whole mess by A) not loaning out the mirror, or B) setting guards of your own on it." I dropped my arms to my sides. "Arrogance is not your friend when it comes to keeping magical artifacts out of the wrong hands."

The rumpled elf continued to glare at me. I ignored her in favor of telling Mr. Whitehaven, "We need to talk to you for a minute."

"Of course." He gestured at the hallway. "My office."

I didn't call Leglin, since he seemed to have our client under control. He'd keep her from eavesdropping.

Once in my boss's office, I explained my immediate personal situation to all three men. There hadn't been time to fill Logan and Dane in between the boss's call and getting to the office.

Before I'd finished, Whitehaven had his elbows planted on his desk, and his head in his hands.

"So," I said, "I kind of have to go back to the demon realm anyway."

"Dear child, you're going to be the death of me."

"I'm sorry, but it would've been nice if someone had mentioned that I shouldn't leave bits of myself anywhere when I began this job." That hadn't come up until I'd been working for nearly a year. "And it's not like it's easy to clean up when you're practically dead."

"She has a point."

"Thanks." I smiled at Logan. "What I'd like to know is, is there a way to search the demon realm that's sneaky? Our frontal assault the first time around almost didn't end well."

"Petra."

Everyone looked at Logan. I said, "What?"

His eyes narrowed, he tapped his leg. "Actually, Tase."

"I'm not taking a baby anything into the demon realm."

Mr. Whitehaven spoke. "I'm afraid you'll have to, if Petra agrees. Gargoyles can sense items that belong to their chosen. Tase will need to be present to help you recover those items."

Fantastic. Look at me, putting my newest, youngest friend in potential danger. "What about the mirror?"

"It wasn't destroyed, therefore the spirit isn't free. Quite likely, the spirit was moved into a new receptacle. I would assume another mirror, as transferring such beings into entirely different surroundings can," Mr. Whitehaven slowly waggled one hand. "Unbalance them."

There was still a chance to recover the Mirror Pervert and throw a wrench into whatever the demons were cooking up. Good. "Okay, but how do we find it?"

"Ooh, I know." Dane lowered his hand once he had our attention. "We take a piece of its old home with us. A gargoyle can track just about anything, if it has the scent."

"And it can get a scent from a mirror?"

"Scent isn't exactly the correct word, but it's close. Gargoyles can make a connection." Logan smiled. "They're better trackers than we are, better than anyone."

"Okay, so I definitely need to go see Petra and ask for her help."

Everyone nodded.

I clapped my hands together. "Then let's go."

For once, the gargoyles were as active as they were supposed to be at night. Apparently, the mourning period was over.

"Lady Discordia." One of the parrot-beaked gargoyles looked down from its position at the top of the walls. "Welcome."

"Hi. We need to talk to Petra, please." I heard the faint grinding noise of the gargoyles' mental communication.

He, or it, blinked and lowered his head, "Our queen will meet with you. Please enter."

"Thank you. Come on, guys." We walked through the gate, closing it behind us, and I saw Petra at the end of the main path, waiting for us. When we were closer, I saw Tase sitting on top of her head.

Prince Tase made a cute crown. I wondered why Petra hadn't mentioned her status before, but now wasn't the time to ask. "Hello, and thank you for seeing us."

"You're welcome. Have you news of the one responsible for the curse?"

I grimaced. "We're pretty sure it's a demon. See, turns out that one got hold of some of my hair and blood."

Petra growled. "Careless of you, allowing that to occur."

"I know that now, but I didn't then. You can bet I'll be a lot more careful in the future." I'd burn any spilled blood, and make certain no one cut my hair other than my hairdresser. I'd burn it, too, though she might think my request to bag the clippings weird.

"See that you do. You'll need my aid to retrieve your missing pieces."

"Yes, ma'am. That's why we're here."

Petra flicked her ears. "Very well. Are these two accompanying us?"

"Yes." Logan and Dane were armed with Mr. Whitehaven's sword and dagger. "My hound can come, too."

"No need. Hounds are unable to move as quickly as we can in the demon realm."

If Leglin couldn't keep up with gargoyles, neither could we. About to point that out, I flinched as two large shapes dropped from above, landing on either side of Petra.

The new arrivals were in shapes I could identify: Gryphons.

"Rake and Rend will serve as your companions' mounts for this foray." Petra inclined her head. "I will be yours."

"Oh. Okay. Thank you." Would we be flying? I hoped not, since none of them wore saddles. "There's something else. We were hired to find and recover an enchanted mirror. We did, but the demons took the spirit it housed and put him in something else."

Petra snorted. "Demons are known thieves. Have you the mirror, or a piece of it?"

"Yes." I pulled the long splinter Logan had shaved off the mirror frame's back from my purse. Petra lifted her paw, so I handed it over.

She ate it.

"Um..."

"We will recover the spirit and return it to the rightful guardian," she said after swallowing it.

"Lady Celadine."

"No. Elves are not the rightful guardians."

I wasn't going to argue with her. The elf could, if she dared. "Who is the rightful guardian?"

"You are."

"Okay, that's … what? I am? I didn't even know about it."

Petra bared one fang in a feline half-smile. "Nevertheless, it tastes of your bloodline. Therefore, you are the rightful guardian."

Still wasn't going to argue with her. "Okay."

"My child's choice becomes ever clearer. Come forward and mount. We must go."

I shot Logan a helpless look. He grinned. "Keep your knees away from her wing joints."

TWENTY-TWO

Gargoyles and shifters aside, I felt sorely undermanned when the tunnel outside the cells appeared around us.

"Stay astride, unless we face a battle," Petra said. She walked a few steps to look inside the open door of the mirror's former cell. "We begin from this point."

I didn't know how she'd picked the spot, since Petra hadn't asked any questions or for directions.

"I knew." Tase left his seat on her head, crawling up on my arm. "I could see it, and showed Mama."

"Oh." If he could see inside my head, things would get really awkward in the future.

The baby gargoyle perched on my shoulder, digging his claws into my jacket. His tail slipped around the back of my neck.

He didn't seem worried. I guess if your mother was an eight-hundred-pound gorilla—so to speak—not much would scare you.

"Alanna is going to be jealous." Dane patted the feathered neck of his gargoyle gryphon. I thought he was riding Rake. "Dad carved her a few dozen gargoyles when we were kids. She still has them."

"That's neat." I tightened my legs as Petra began walking. The tunnel wasn't wide enough for us all to travel side by side, but the other two gargoyles could, behind her.

We were the head of a three-gargoyle arrow. Whoopee.

"I sense the mirror." Petra sniffed. "And your missing pieces."

The way she said that made me want to count my fingers and toes. Maybe arms and legs, too. "Great."

My intention was to burn my "pieces" as soon as possible. I'd have to figure out what to do with the mirror or whatever the spirit was in now. I doubted Lady Celadine would be pleased to learn it wasn't hers. Not that I considered it mine, or wanted to be in charge of a trapped spirit. I had enough trouble keeping myself in one piece.

Hey, maybe I could use the spirit as a bribe, to shut down Thorandryll's pursuit of me. The idea was more amusing than riding a gargoyle down demon realm tunnels.

Even better if the spirit found Prince Snooty pants attractive.

Who was I kidding? The mirror spirit was a problem. "You said the mirror tasted of my bloodline."

"Yes."

"I was told a god trapped the spirit in the mirror. So does that mean an ancestor made the mirror, or that the spirit is an ancestor of mine?"

"No."

I waited, but Petra didn't explain. "If both of those possibilities are a no, then how can it taste of my bloodline?"

Tase giggled. "You're silly."

"Guess so, because I don't understand what the deal is."

"Don't you know anything about your family lineage?" He patted me right in front of my ear. "You're a natural mage."

"So I've been told."

"Natural mages are descended from the gods."

Which meant... "The god that stuffed the spirit in the mirror is my ancestor."

"Of course." Petra paused to study the intersection of tunnels we'd reached. "One of them. You're descended from more than one."

Kethyrdryll had told me that, based on the fact I had several abilities. "Do you know which god did it?"

"Cernunnos."

I looked back, meeting Logan's eyes. He and Dane both looked surprised. "Seriously? I'm related to that scary dude?"

"Many thousands of years ago," Petra said. "Though the rapid breeding of humanoids does suggest you're related to Cernunnos many times over."

"How?"

"The great families had many children. Some of those children interbred with one another, through alliances. Others bred with untalented humans, or other humanoid species." Petra went straight. "It's unlikely at this point in time that you'd be able to find anyone unrelated to you, or anyone else, should you delve deeply enough into their bloodlines."

"Oh." That actually made sense, considering the sheer number of people alive in the world now, compared to thousands of years in the past. "Any chance you know which other gods I'm related to, way back when?"

Another intersection passed before Petra answered. She went right that time. "You can discover that yourself, by comparing your talents with those of the gods. Each great family began with the children who inherited similar gifts from their godly parents."

I had a feeling learning to make spreadsheets was in my near future. "Okay, so since I have electrokinesis, that means I'm related to, say, Zeus?"

"Yes, and other gods who favored wielding lightning." Petra was turning her head from side to side and carefully sniffing the air.

"But a really long time ago."

"Of course." She immediately dropped a bomb on me. "Which is interesting, considering the lack of dilution in your bloodline."

"I'm sorry, what?" I looked back again, only to receive shrugs from the guys.

"I believe you may be the product of an intensive breeding program."

Mind reeling, I waited a few minutes before asking the most obvious question. "Why do you think that?"

"After two thousand years of split realms, the mere existence of a multi-talented natural mage of your power cannot be simple happenstance."

"Awesome." My stomach lurched, and I could feel the start of a headache forming. "It couldn't have been too intensive after the Sundering, though."

Petra laughed, or that's what I thought the low, grinding noise she uttered was. "The gods act in mysterious ways."

That gave me more food for thought than I felt capable of digesting.

TWENTY-THREE

The only conversation after that was Petra's muttering about how close we were getting with every new turn.

Even I could tell we'd traveled steadily downward, thanks to the pressure building in my ears. Yet we hadn't come across a single demon. "Anyone else feel like we may be walking into a trap?"

"That thought did cross my mind." Dane smiled when I glanced back. "But we're in great company, if we are."

"Good to know, as long as everyone knows I can't do anything down here. Oh, except scream and bleed."

Logan chuckled. "You have a gargoyle guardian. You'll be fine."

I reached up to pat Tase's side. "Right."

My tiny guardian purred in response, which kept me from saying anything that might offend him. He was a baby, not a full-grown gargoyle.

But his mother was. As long as Tase was attached to me, I probably didn't have to worry about Petra keeping me in one piece, especially since she'd basically promised to.

"All items are together," Petra said. "And we are but a moment away from them."

She moved to the side, allowing the other two gargoyles to pass us in single file. Logan and Dane wore identical, grim smiles, and each saluted us with their borrowed weapons.

Smart, having the people who could do damage go first. I felt pretty useless. What was the good of being allegedly descended from gods, if I couldn't do a damn thing down here?

Petra followed Rake and Rend—who I hoped would live up to their names—and Tase readjusted his position to snuggle against my neck.

I didn't complain about the grip he took on my hair. Whatever made him feel secure.

A turn came into view, and when we made it, there was much brighter light at the end of the tunnel. I gulped and whispered, "Here goes nothing."

Tase giggled, but I felt him shiver. Was he scared, or was he picking up on my fears?

I wasn't used to being helpless, and wished I'd thought to bring my gun. Preferably loaded with demon-banishing potion.

Wait, that was a pretty cool idea. I needed to run it by the witches, see if it was a worthwhile idea.

Wow, what if we made wooden bullets? Would they ash vampires?

And why was I being inundated with such cool ideas now?

Rake and Rend entered the lit area, and a second later, so did we.

"How pleasant of you to join us." The blonde woman from my vision smiled. She stood behind a heavy, wooden table. A stone bowl sat before her, and she held an antique-looking, tarnished silver hand mirror. "I've been tracking your progress."

She wasn't alone, and the dozen or so demons waiting with her weren't wearing human facades. One of them looked like the demon who'd killed Thorandryll's thieving ex-girlfriend by raping her to death.

I barely kept from peeing myself, and on Petra, at the sight of him standing there, larger than all the other demons.

"Party crashers, we're not," Dane said. "That takes out some of the fun."

Petra moved between the two gryphon gargoyles. "We are here to retrieve items belonging to my ward."

"No, you're here to facilitate our plans. I will give our terms only once: Leave this place without the woman. We need her."

Petra cocked her head. "For what purpose?"

"Gargoyles are curious creatures. Her death will open a permanent gateway to the world above. We'll control that gateway, and by proxy, our entire realm." The blonde lifted and turned the mirror, revealing the spirits' pale green face. "The living grimoire has been quite helpful."

"Freaking jerk. No wonder Cernunnos stuffed you in a mirror." Scowling, I pointed at him. It. What the hell ever. "You just made my list, buddy. The Smash It one."

"Sorry, babe. Smashing me isn't a good idea, since no one knows what'll happen."

"Then I'll think of something else."

Tase murmured into my ear. "Your hair and blood are in that bowl."

"You guys missed your chance to sacrifice me. The time for it to work has passed."

"True, for the reworked spell. This one's different."

Fantastic. How many freaking spells were there that needed me dead as the final ingredient?

"My ward is not yours to use," Petra said. "I have no preference for a peaceful resolution to this situation."

"Neither do I. We only need her alive. Kill the rest." The blonde placed the mirror on the table, next to the bowl.

Sincerely wishing I could teleport right then, I swallowed a scream as the demons rushed toward us.

Petra didn't move. Rake and Rend did, the second Logan and Dane slid off their backs. The gryphon gargoyles tore into the advancing demons with hawk-like screams.

"Dismount," Petra ordered, and I reluctantly obeyed. "Stay here."

She bounded forward, past Logan and Dane, who'd ganged up on a mottled red and black demon.

One of the gryphons shot into the air, its beak tearing into the throat of the demon clutched in its claws. Blood splattered everywhere as Rake, or Rend, dismembered the demon before diving for another victim.

The demon's arm plopped down in front of me, fingers twitching. I stared at it. "Tase?"

"Yes?"

"Have you learned anything about demon blood?"

He moved slightly. "A little. It's a necessary ingredient for some potions and spells."

"I was told that if I drank some, I'd be able to use my abilities down here. Do you know anything about that?"

"No. Who told you that?"

"A god."

"Oh."

"So you wouldn't know if there'd be any side effects."

Tase winced as his mother roared. I checked for her, and found her squaring off with a putrid green demon.

"No. I'm sorry."

"It's okay." I debated for a minute, then crouched down and dragged two fingers through the pool of blood forming at the arm's severed end.

I made the mistake of sniffing my bloody fingers first. "Oh, gag. That's awful."

"It is demon blood."

"Yeah." Steeling myself, I opened my mouth and stuck my fingers in. The blood tasted like rotting meat. I fought to swallow it, and then to keep from throwing up. "This had better work, because I'm not doing that again."

"Mama said to stay here."

"We don't," I gagged, regained control, and finished with, "have to move. I can do what I need to from here."

Closing my eyes, I concentrated on focusing on the recent memory of where the bowl containing my "pieces" was located. I had to use memory, since I couldn't see the table through the snarl of demons, gargoyles, and shifters.

A scream opened my eyes, and struck a temporary lull in the battle. "Oops, I went a little overboard."

Smoke was pouring from the bowl, my intended target. Flames were devouring the blonde's scarlet robes as she writhed. "Guess she's not flame retardant."

With my "pieces" destroyed, it felt like the time had come to leave. "Tell your mom..."

"She already knows," Tase said. "She's going to collect the mirror."

Oh, yeah. We probably shouldn't leave that behind. I shrieked as a demon broke from the melee, heading straight for us.

It was the same son-of-a-bitch who'd murdered and eaten Carole. The one who'd seen me during the vision I'd had of her "sacrifice".

My insides turned to water and I forgot I had the use of my abilities as it charged, knocking Logan aside with its tail when he followed.

"Holy crap."

Logan flew through the air, twisted, and hit the wall feet first. He rebounded, landing on the floor in a roll, and was on his feet.

But he wasn't going to reach us in time to do anything.

Tase whimpered.

Right, I had to do something, and the lingering taste of rotten meat reminded me that I could.

I went for my electrokinesis, which responded by surging out. Blue-white lightning crawled down my arms, and I raised them, aiming my palms at the oncoming demon. Thick, flickering ropes of electricity shot from my hands, and my hair rose, crackling.

All that blue-white power struck the big demon dead center, and next thing I knew, I was on my ass in the tunnel, watching a rain of charred demon bits falling inside the room.

"Wow." Tase crawled down my chest. His mane was standing on end, full of static. "You blew it up."

"Uh huh." My hair wasn't in any better shape. I tried to smooth it down, but it only clung to my hands.

Tase leaped to sit on my knee. "I hope that's all you blew up."

Me too. "I still hear some fighting."

"Cordi?" Logan appeared in the tunnel's opening, covered in lightly fried demon gore. "You okay?"

"Think so. Headache building."

Dane appeared next, and he was laughing. "Boom!" was the only word I made out.

"Glad I was able to entertain you." I scooped Tase off my knee and climbed to my feet. "Did we win?"

"The gargoyles are finishing off the last few demons," Logan said.

"Good. I'm ready to leave." I spat. "Ugh, can't get rid of the taste."

"How'd you do that?"

"Sal told me I could use my abilities down here if I ingested some demon blood. He was correct." I spat again. "Demon blood tastes friggin' horrible, if you ever wondered."

"I already know, and, fair warning: It'll be days before you quit tasting it."

My groan set Dane to laughing again.

"Mom says to come back." Tase climbed to my shoulder.

"Okay." We left the tunnel, re-entering the room, and paused to survey the carnage. Pieces of twitching demons were strewn about, lying in pools of blood. My stomach heaved, and I couldn't keep from reacting. Tase lunged free as I bent down and threw up a bloody mess of my own.

Demon blood didn't taste better on the return trip.

Finished, I wiped my mouth on my jacket sleeve and straightened, wishing I had some dignity left to gather. "Can we go now?"

"Yes." Petra brandished the spirit's new home in one huge paw. "This is yours."

The spirit took one look at me and faded from sight. I grinned. "Yeah, hiding's a good idea, jackass."

The gargoyles took us to the office's parking lot, immediately disappearing once we dismounted. I was not happy to discover our client was still present when we went inside.

"You recovered my property. I'm shocked." Celadine attempted to snatch the mirror from me.

I smacked her hand away. "No, you don't."

"It's mine." Her beautiful face turned feral. Teeth bared, she made another grab.

I gave her a telekinetic shove. "According to the queen of the gargoyles, it's not yours. It's mine, and I'm going to keep it."

Celadine whirled to face Mr. Whitehaven. "Order her to return my property."

"If Queen Petra stated the spirit belongs to Discordia, I am not going to believe otherwise."

"Of all the," Celadine turned back. "You have no right."

I sighed, and made a face as the gust of my breath caused a renewal of the rotten meat taste. "I'm really tired of elves trying to tell me what to do. You should stop before you piss me off."

"Really should. Gods and demons tend to go boom when Cordi's pissed." Dane grinned. "And I do mean Boom."

The elf sniffed. "She wouldn't dare."

"Yeah, I would. I mean, you're just an elf. I, however, am descended from gods. A lot of them, from what I've learned, including Cernunnos." I leaned forward, staring into her eyes. "So get the hell out of my face."

To my surprise, Celadine paled and disappeared. "Wow. That worked."

"You were quite menacing." Mr. Whitehaven smiled. "Are any of you injured?"

"Bumps and bruises. I have a headache."

"And we all need showers," Logan said.

"Excellent work." The boss inclined his head. "What of your personal issue?"

"Taken care of, and believe me, I'll be a lot more careful about bleeding, and haircuts, in the future."

"Good plan." Dane patted my shoulder. "Mind giving us a lift home?"

"My work is never done."

TWENTY-FOUR

The next morning, I skipped jogging in favor of scrubbing my mouth several times. It didn't help. I could still taste rotten meat, but not as strongly.

Downstairs, I made coffee and took the dogs outside, before deciding I'd put off the mirror problem long enough. Having left it shiny side down on the dinette table the night before, I sat down with a fresh cup of coffee and turned it over.

All I saw was my own reflection. "Hey."

No response.

"Look, dude, I'm really not in the mood for your crap. Show yourself right now, or I'll hand you over to Cernunnos."

Green blazed, and the spirit glared at me. "That's not a nice thing to say."

"Newsflash, I'm not interested in being nice to someone who tried to sell me out to demons."

His face scrunched. "They were in possession of me. I have to obey the one who possesses me."

"Uh huh." I glared back. "You're a freaking grimoire."

"Well, yes. It's not as though I had a choice. I've had a long line of owners, all of whom chose to share their magical knowledge with me. I am what Cernunnos made me."

Ouch. I had the feeling that meant we probably had some common ground, if what Petra believed was true, about my being a product of godly tampering. "Okay, I'm going to suggest we call a truce."

"A truce." The spirit's eyes narrowed. "All right, what's the catch?"

"No catch."

"Well, I must say, that's a first. There's always been a catch before, in my dealings with previous owners."

"Okay, one catch. Don't call me 'babe' ever again."

A deep laugh rolled out of the mirror. "Agreed."

"Thanks." I touched the metal frame of the mirror. "Is it crowded in there? This is like an efficiency apartment, compared to your old digs."

He laughed again. "I have all the space I need, but it's nice you're concerned."

"You're welcome. I have to decide what to do with you. I can't keep you here. Celadine will probably come hunting for you."

"Possession does equal access to all my secrets." He paused. "Eventually, of course. This is a boring afterlife. I have to entertain myself somehow."

I nodded. "I have possession now. Does that mean you'll tell me all your secrets?"

All the laughter drained from his greenish face, leaving it a solemn oblong. "If you wish."

"Could you tell me who Sal really is?"

"That's not my secret to tell. I will tell you he's been known as the Nameless God for centuries. Furthermore, I'll say to hold me as a warning against meddling in the plans of gods."

A shiver rolled down my spine, even though I already knew how he'd gotten into the mirror. There were probably worse fates, but being disembodied and trapped in an inanimate object had to be in the Top Twenty Ways I Didn't Want to Die, Yet Live Forever. "I could destroy the mirror. What would happen to you if I did that?"

"As I told you last night, no one knows. Perhaps I'd finally, truly die. Perhaps not." He blinked. "The uncertainty is unpleasant."

"Well, I can't keep you. I'm human. Temptation usually becomes a problem for us in the right circumstances."

"For someone as young as you are, you do have moments of extreme wisdom."

"I trust Mr. Whitehaven, but someone could find out I gave you to him. I don't want to cause any trouble for him."

"You could present me to the Nameless God," he suggested.

"Uh uh. He's got enough power."

"Your coven of witch friends?"

"Once they know you're a grimoire, they'll destroy you."

"Prince Thorandryll?"

"Get real."

He laughed again. "You could hide me away in your clan territory."

"Nope, that puts them in danger." I sighed. "Running out of possibilities. Oh, wait. The gargoyles?"

"They're stone half the time. Anyone could steal me while they sleep, and one willing to risk their wrath isn't someone you want possessing me."

Good point. I wished everything didn't have to be so damned hard. That's when an idea flew into my head. "The dragon."

"Hm." He considered the idea before giving a slow nod. "Yes. That's a good solution."

"Right? No one will try to steal you from him, if anyone ever found out. He's not human or an elf." Plus, he was extremely old, and wasn't interested in ruling the world—or blowing it up. At least as far as I knew, and I suspected that if Lord Kadon had a world domination plan, everyone would know about it by now. "You'll be safe with him."

"And the world will be safe from me." An arch smile rounded his lean cheeks.

"Yes, that too. Sorry."

"Child, you played no part in what I've become. I bear you no ill will, and were I in your place, I'd make the same decision. The world has enough problems."

"Maybe I can visit you once in a while." I felt bad, planning to lock him away. Maybe he wasn't alive in the accepted sense of the word, but he was a person. A dangerous one, in the wrong hands.

"If you do, bring magazines. The sexy ones." He waggled his bushy eyebrows.

"You are such a pervert."

"Please?"

I rolled my eyes. "Okay. I need to make a phone call."

Teleportation had long past become my favorite ability. It's hard to keep track of someone who can disappear before you can blink.

I stood between the two stunted pines Mr. Whitehaven had described to me, facing a small hill, with a light breeze ruffling my hair and chilling my cheeks. The mirror was tucked inside my jacket. His muffled complaints about not being higher and facing my chest were a little hard to ignore. "Would you shut up? There will be no motor boating. Where did you even learn about that?"

"Premium channels. I learned oh, so much from..."

"I didn't need to know. Really. It wasn't a serious question. Now shush." He subsided and I looked around, making certain we were alone. All I saw was a jackrabbit hopping away. "Okay. Hello? It's Discord Jones, sir."

The little hill's front shimmered and faded away, revealing a dark entrance. Warm air flowed from it, a single word riding that breeze. "Enter."

"Thank you." I had to bend to go inside, but a few steps later, could stand without worrying I'd bump my noggin. The light went out as the entrance closed behind me.

I stayed put, the darkness complete, and could hear my blood pounding in my ears within a few seconds. The dragon's deep voice startled me. "Why have you come?"

"To give you something I don't think will be safe with anyone else."

"The mirror spirit."

It wasn't a question. "Yes, sir. How did you know I had it?"

With a whoosh, flames came to life around me. I blinked to adjust my vision. The fires were torches, mounted on brown, stone walls.

Lord Kadon sat before me, in actual dragon shape, and smaller than I'd thought he'd be, from Terra's description. His spade-tipped tail curled around his front legs, reminding me of a cat. A horse-sized, dragon-shaped cat.

"You're mortal. Mortals have difficulties destroying things of power."

That sounded like a condemnation to me. "It seemed safer not to burn it, because I didn't know what would happen."

"Sensible. You sound offended. I knew greed for power wasn't the reason, child. If it had been, you wouldn't be here."

I pulled the mirror out of my jacket and held it up. "Nope, I wouldn't be. I have enough power on my plate, thanks."

"Bring it closer." The dragon stood and turned in a sinuous circle. I followed as he led the way to a tunnel at the back of the cave. The tunnel was larger than the short distance had been.

Torches flickered to life ahead of him as we walked. Their light didn't pierce the blackness of the entrances dotting either side. I kept looking at each anyway, wondering what lay beyond them.

My curiosity caught me stepping on the dragon's tail when he stopped. "Oops. Sorry."

He flicked his tail out from under my foot when I lifted it. "In here."

We turned right, into one of those entrances, and torches inside the new tunnel came to life. It ended in a square room with stony shelves carved into the walls.

"Place it on the empty stand, next to that sword."

"Yes, sir." Careful not to step on his tail, I did as ordered. The mirror grinned once he was in place.

"Don't forget the magazines."

"I won't." I glanced at the sword, which was a plain, straight thing with a leather-wrapped grip. It didn't even have a jewel in the pommel. "That doesn't look like a treasure piece."

Smoke scented the air as Lord Kadon chuffed. He moved his head, which came to a stop beside me. "Beauty is in the eye of the beholder, child. That plain sword is quite famous among humans. It belonged to a king whose days were marred by tragedy. He died with it in his hand, after charging a loyal companion to return it from whence it came."

I hadn't read many stories where a sword was that important. In fact, only one came to mind, and it fit what he'd said. "Are you telling me that's Excalibur?"

"Yes."

"Holy cow." Respect filled me as I eyed the sword. "May I touch it?"

"You may lift it down, if you're able."

My fingers were twitching, but I hesitated. "What do you mean?"

"Excalibur will refuse to bend to the will of any it judges unworthy."

"Oh." Maybe I didn't want to touch the sword. What if it decided I was unworthy? I wasn't sure what that would do to my self-esteem, being deemed unworthy by a legendary, magical sword.

"Go ahead," the dragon said. "I confess to a certain curiosity in the outcome."

Crap. I was his guest. It'd be rude to refuse to try. "Okay."

Excalibur wasn't on a stand. It lay on a long cushion of royal purple velvet. I slid my hands under the grip and blade. It felt warm. I whispered, "Moment of truth."

Lord Kadon's soft chuckle didn't exactly boost my confidence. My tentative lift shifted the sword's position. "Ooh."

I lifted it higher and stepped back with a grin. "Pretty sure I just gained a thousand coolness points. It's not as heavy as I thought it would be."

My host had moved away from the shelf, too. "Excalibur adjusts to its bearer."

"Nifty." I moved my hand from the blade to the grip, the sword pointing up. The grip was made for a pair of larger hands, yet felt light enough to use one-handed. I resisted the urge to swing it around. "Awesome. Crossing 'meet Excalibur' off my bucket list now."

Not that it'd been on my list, but I had more than a few items I'd added and instantly crossed off.

After turning Excalibur this way and that to watch it gleam in the light, I returned it to the cushion. With a final pat to the guard, I said, "It was nice to meet you, and thanks for the vote of confidence."

"You don't wish to keep the sword?"

"Who, me?" I turned, surprise widening my eyes. "What, like a trade? Mirror for sword?"

"You were allowed to lift it, thus Excalibur deems you worthy of bearing it."

My head turned and I touched the flat of the blade. "I appreciate the compliment, but I don't know how to use a sword. You'd end up in the top of my closet, to keep anyone from trying to steal you."

The dragon chuffed, smoke puffing from his nostrils. "Excalibur can't be stolen. Thieves won't be able to move it."

"Oh, right. Duh." I pulled my fingers away and shook my head. "I'd better not. It's not the sort of thing you display as a conversation piece, and I'd look silly carrying it around everywhere."

He inclined his head. "As you wish. Though, should you find a need for it, come to see me. As long as Excalibur deems you worthy, you may use it."

Me, chosen by possibly the most famous sword in the world. My brain couldn't handle that much awesome. I fell back on the courtesies Mom had drilled into me. "Thank you."

"Come now."

I followed Lord Kadon out of the room, and all the way back to the cave. Didn't step on his tail again, despite trying to peek into the other dark openings along our way.

If he had Excalibur, there was no telling what else he had. Maybe the wardrobe that led to Narnia or the rabbit hole Alice had fallen down. A unicorn? My mind was bouncing all over the place.

When the dragon sat, I walked around to the entrance tunnel, but turned to ask, "Do you ever give tours of your treasure trove?"

"Rarely."

"Oh. Okay. Well, thank you for letting me visit, and for agreeing to take the mirror." I hesitated. "I told him I'd visit, if I could. Would that be okay? I mean, not every week or anything like that..."

"Why would you wish to visit such a troublesome object?"

"So he won't get too lonely. He's a person."

"The spirit of a once-living person," he corrected.

"Okay, sure, but he's still kind of alive. It's mean to just lock him away."

"Very well, you may visit ... him." His eyes twinkled, probably an effect of the torchlight. "And perhaps I will allow you to see more of my collection."

"That would be fantastic. Thank you. I guess I'd better go. Need to get ready for my date."

"You're welcome." Sunlight spilled around me. Before I turned to leave, the dragon added, "Tell your young man hello for me."

"I will. Bye." With a smile, I turned and walked down the entry tunnel, not having to duck my head this time. The entrance was gone when I looked over my shoulder to check after clearing it. "Cool."

I swiveled again to make sure nobody was there to witness me winking out to teleport home. The ant trundling across the toe of my boot seemed innocuous enough.

Things hadn't turned out all that bad. I was free of my curse-caused Merriven delusions, Logan and I were finally dating, and I'd even gotten to scare the crap out of an elf.

Life was pretty damn good.

Taking a deep breath, I had to smile, and immediately grimaced at the taste of rotten meat.

Good, except for that. Ugh.

About the Author

A sword-toting alien with a fetish for fur and four-legged creatures, she writes fiction and spends entirely too much time distracted by shiny things online, like Twitter.

She prefers Netflix because there aren't any commercials and she can ignore all the reality series. As a voracious reader, she enjoys both ebooks and physical books, though her ebook collection doesn't require regular dusting.

She writes scifi as G. L. Drummond, fantasy as Gayla Drummond, and other things as Louise Drummond.

If you're interested in news and future releases, you can find her on Facebook (http://www.facebook.com/G.L.Drummond), Twitter (@Scath), or visit her author web site at http://gldrummond.com.

The Discord Jones urban fantasy series has its own web site at http://discordjones.com.